At Issue

Is America a Democracy or an Oligarchy?

Other Books in the At Issue Series

COVID-19 and Other Pandemics
Food Security
Genocide
The Media's Influence on Society
Money Laundering
Nuclear Anxiety
Open Borders
Partisanship
Policing in America
The Politicization of the Supreme Court

Is America a Democracy or an Oligarchy?

Eamon Doyle, Book Editor

Published in 2022 by Greenhaven Publishing, LLC
353 3rd Avenue, Suite 255, New York, NY 10010

Copyright © 2022 by Greenhaven Publishing, LLC

First Edition

All rights reserved. No part of this book may be reproduced in any form without permission in writing from the publisher, except by a reviewer.

Articles in Greenhaven Publishing anthologies are often edited for length to meet page requirements. In addition, original titles of these works are changed to clearly present the main thesis and to explicitly indicate the author's opinion. Every effort is made to ensure that Greenhaven Publishing accurately reflects the original intent of the authors. Every effort has been made to trace the owners of the copyrighted material.

Cover image: PEPPERSMINT/Shutterstock.com

Library of Congress Cataloging-in-Publication Data
Names: Doyle, Eamon, 1988- editor.
Title: Is America a democracy or an oligarchy? / Eamon Doyle, book editor.
Description: First edition. | New York : Greenhaven Publishing, 2022. |
    Series: At issue | Includes bibliographical references and index. |
    Audience: Ages 15+ | Audience: Grades 10–12 | Summary: "Anthology of viewpoints
    that examine the development of the United States from political,
    social, and economic perspectives to determine whether the country can
    still be considered a democracy."— Provided by publisher.
Identifiers: LCCN 2020051419 | ISBN 9781534508156 (library binding) | ISBN
    9781534508149 (paperback) | ISBN 9781534508255 (ebook)
Subjects: LCSH: Democracy—Economic aspects—United States—Juvenile
    literature. | Oligarchy—United States—Juvenile literature. | United
    States—Politics and government—Juvenile literature.
Classification: LCC JK1726 .I77 2022 | DDC 330.973—dc23
LC record available at https://lccn.loc.gov/2020051419

Manufactured in the United States of America

Website: http://greenhavenpublishing.com

Contents

Introduction	7
1. Oligarchy in Theory and Practice *Kimberly Amadeo*	11
2. Income Inequality in the United States *Matthew Johnston*	17
3. Inequality Is a Threat to Democracy *The Guardian*	22
4. Democracy Doesn't Guarantee Economic Liberty *Arthur Foulkes*	25
5. Inequality Has Resulted in a Populist Surge *Michael Sandel*	31
6. The Politics of Progressive Reform in the United States *Daniel T. Rodgers*	42
7. Corporate Capture Threatens Democratic Government *Liz Kennedy*	52
8. Privatization and Corporate Wealth in the Late Twentieth Century *Sarah Anderson and John Cavanagh*	58
9. We Should Be Investing in People and Things Other Than War *Jake Johnson*	69
10. The US Has a Government of, by, and for Billionaires *Bernie Sanders*	77
11. The Case for Democratic Socialism in the United States *Bhaskar Sunkara*	84
12. Approaching Oligarchy in the Legal System *Rebecca Buckwalter-Poza*	88
13. Labor Unions Still Matter in America *Jake Rosenfeld*	101
14. Populism Is No Match for the Elite Establishment *Dan Sanchez*	106
Organizations to Contact	113
Bibliography	120
Index	124

Introduction

Democracy is commonly understood to mean "government of and by the people." In other words, the basic idea of a democratic system is to invest regular citizens with a degree of power over how and by whom they are governed. This power is what distinguishes democratic governance from, for instance, the unmitigated power held by a dictator in an authoritarian state or a king in a monarchical system.

In the contemporary world, most democracies operate based on systems of elected representation wherein citizens' participatory power is represented by a right to vote in free elections; citizens elect representatives to serve in official positions and to advance their interests as much as possible while doing so. (The catch for the politicians is that if they fail to protect their constituents' interests while in office, they are likely to lose their position in the next election.) It's a straightforward idea, but the reality quickly becomes more complicated when you consider the broader context of an electoral system, a capitalist economy, political parties, and the various ways in which these and other peripheral dynamics interact. Such complexity ensures that no two democracies or elections are exactly alike.

Indeed, the modern world contains examples of socialist democracies, liberal democracies, and illiberal democracies, as well as democratic activity ranging from radical to conservative, populist to aristocratic, progressive to libertarian. The democratic ideal is broad enough to encompass all such political diversity—so long as elections are free and fair, and elected officials' primary incentive is to serve the interests of their constituents. Democracy in America has certainly seen more than its share of political and ideological diversity. In recent years, however, some concerned observers have argued that contemporary America has drifted from its democratic bearings and now more closely resembles an entirely different form of government: oligarchy.

If we think of democracy as government of and by the people, then we can think of oligarchy as government of and by the few—usually wealthy and well-connected elites. Kimberly Amadeo, president of WorldMoneyWatch and author of 2010's *Beyond the Great Recession*, defines oligarchy in the following terms:

> *An oligarchy is a power structure that allows a few businesses, families, or individuals to rule. Those few ruling members have enough power to create policies that benefit them to the exclusion of the rest of society. They maintain their power through their relationships with each other. [...] They become an organized minority, while average citizens remain an unorganized majority. The oligarchs groom protégés who share their values and goals. It becomes more difficult for the average person to break into the group of elites.*

Pundits who argue that the United States is closer to an oligarchy than a democracy usually begin by throwing a spotlight on wealth inequality and, in parallel with Amadeo's latter point, declining economic mobility.

But what do income inequality and economic mobility have to do with democratic politics? In an editorial published in the *Guardian*, Yale University political scientist Jacob Hacker and his colleague Nathaniel Loewentheil examined what happens to democracy when massive wealth inequality coincides with private campaign funding:

> *Money doesn't just give big spenders the chance to express a view or support a candidate; it gives them leverage to reshape the American economy in their favor. And as the richest have pulled away from the rest of America, the policies they want—extremely low tax rates on the wealthy at a time of record deficits, rampant underinvestment in our future, special treatment for corporations that are imposing major environmental costs and financial risks on our society—are increasingly at odds with the policies the country desperately needs.*

Introduction

This analysis puts a spotlight on the basic problem raised by contemporary observers of American politics: When an ostensibly democratic system struggles to respond to urgent popular imperatives and instead primarily serves the interests of a donor class, the nature of the political environment has fundamentally changed.

This isn't the first time that observers have questioned the democratic integrity of the US political system in this way. The late nineteenth and early twentieth century—an era that historians often refer to as "the Gilded Age"—saw massive concentrations of private wealth and business titans who used that wealth to gain access, favor, and influence with the political leaders of the time. Citizens and political activists viewed these conditions as a threat to democracy and organized to push for reforms. Consequently, the Gilded Age in the United States was followed by a period known as the Progressive Era, during which a more populist concept of democracy rose to prominence. The Princeton historian Daniel T. Rodgers elaborates:

> *More than in most eras, Americans in the first years of the twentieth century felt the newness of their place in history. Looking back on the late nineteenth century, they stressed its chaos: the boom-and-bust cycles of the economy, the violent and exploitative aspects of its economy and social life, the gulf between its ostentatious new wealth and the lot of its urban poor and hard-pressed farmers, and the inefficiency of American politics in a world of great nations. […] To break what they saw as the corrupt alliance between business wealth and political party bosses, progressive reformers succeeded in moving the election of US Senators from the state legislatures to the general electorate and, in some states, instituting new systems of popular referenda, initiative, and recall. They championed votes for women, bringing the last states holding out against women's suffrage into line in the Nineteenth Amendment in 1920.*

There are a number of obvious differences between the political and economic conditions of the late nineteenth century and those of the past several decades, but there are also uncanny similarities. Americans concerned about the specter of oligarchy in contemporary US politics might find inspiration by looking back to the reforms and populist spirit of the Progressive Era, when democracy asserted itself against oligarchy—and won the day. These and other issues are explored by the authors of the diverse viewpoints in *At Issue: Is America a Democracy or an Oligarchy?*

1

Oligarchy in Theory and Practice

Kimberly Amadeo

Kimberly Amadeo is president of WorldMoneyWatch and author of several books, including The Ultimate Obamacare Handbook *(2015) and* Beyond the Great Recession *(2010).*

In this short piece, economic expert Kimberly Amadeo reviews the basic concept of oligarchy, including its benefits and drawbacks, and examines both contemporary and historical examples. It is said that all societies will eventually become oligarchies because those in power will always enjoy the advantages and privileges afforded them. While oligarchies result in and thrive on inequality and status quo, they also promote innovation.

An oligarchy is a power structure that allows a few businesses, families, or individuals to rule. Those few ruling members have enough power to create policies that benefit them to the exclusion of the rest of society.

They maintain their power through their relationships with each other. The term "oligarchy" comes from the Greek word *oligarchia*, and it means "few governing."[1]

Three of the most well-known countries with oligarchies are Russia, China, and Iran. Other examples are Saudi Arabia, Turkey, and apartheid-era South Africa.[2]

"Oligarchies, Their Pros and Cons, with Causes and Examples," by Kimberly Amadeo, Dotdash Publishing Family, February 18, 2020. Reprinted by permission.

A plutocracy is a subset of an oligarchy. In a plutocracy, the leaders are rich. The leaders in an oligarchy don't have to be rich, even though they usually are. For example, a high school ruled by a popular clique is an oligarchy. A plutocracy is always an oligarchy, but there could be some oligarchies that aren't plutocracies.

Traits of an Oligarchy

The "iron law of oligarchy" states that any organization or society will eventually become an oligarchy. That's because the people who learn how to succeed in the organization gain a competitive advantage. The larger and more complicated the organization becomes, the more advantages the elite gain.[3]

Oligarchs only associate with others who share those same traits. They become an organized minority, while average citizens remain an unorganized majority. The oligarchs groom protégés who share their values and goals. It becomes more difficult for the average person to break into the group of elites. The following pros and cons summarize some of the benefits and issues:

Pros of an Oligarchy

Oligarchies exist in any organization that delegates power to a group of expert insiders so that the organization can function. It's not efficient for everyone to make all the decisions all the time.

An oligarchy allows most people to focus on their day-to-day lives without too much involvement in the issues that concern society as a whole. They can spend their time doing other things, such as working on their chosen career, cultivating relationships with their families, or engaging in sports.

Oligarchies can make innovation possible, as well. Because the oligarchy manages society, creative people can spend the time needed to invent new technologies. Of course, these creatives will only be successful so long as their inventions and success benefit the oligarchy's interests as well.

The decisions made by an oligarchy are inherently conservative since the goal is to preserve the status quo (keep the ruling class in power). Therefore, it's unlikely that any single leader can steer an oligarchical society into ventures that are too risky.

Cons of an Oligarchy

Oligarchies increase income inequality. That's because the oligarchs siphon a nation's wealth into their pockets. That leaves less for everyone else and fosters greater social inequalities as well. As the insider group gains power, it seeks to keep it. As their knowledge and expertise grow, it becomes more difficult for anyone else to break in.[1]

Oligarchies can become stale. They pick people who share the same values and worldviews and this can sow the seeds of decline since they can miss the profitable synergies of a diverse team.

If an oligarchy takes too much power, it can restrict a free market. For example, members of the oligarchy could agree informally to fix prices, which violates the laws of supply and demand.

If people lose hope that they can one day join the oligarchy, they may become frustrated and violent. Consequently, they may attempt to overthrow the ruling class. This can disrupt the economy and cause pain and suffering for everyone.

How Oligarchies Rise

The people in charge are good at what they do—they wouldn't have risen to that level otherwise. That's how they can continue to take more wealth and power from those who don't have those skills or interests.

An oligarchy forms when leaders agree to increase their power regardless of whether it benefits society. This can happen in any political system.

If the leader is weak, an oligarchy can form under a monarchy or tyranny. An influential group increases its power around this person, and when the leader leaves, the oligarchs remain in power. They select a puppet or one of their own to replace the leader.

Oligarchies can also arise in a democracy if people don't stay informed. This happens more often when a society becomes extremely complex and difficult to understand. People are willing to make the trade-off of ceding power to those with the passion and knowledge to rule—or they simply don't see an alternative.[4]

US Oligarchies

Is the United States an oligarchy? One troubling sign is that income inequality is worsening. Upper-income households in the US enjoyed a 64% income increase in the past half-century, from a median annual income of $126,100 in 1970 to $207,400 in 2018. In that same timeframe, median middle-class income increased just 49% to $86,600, and median lower-income household income grew 43% to $28,700.

As a result, the share of aggregate income going to upper-income households increased from 29% in 1970 to 48% in 2018, while the share for middle-class households fell from 62% to 43%.[5]

Upper-income households represent an elite class of executives, investors, and aristocrats. They go to the same schools, travel in the same social circles, and sit on each others' boards. However, if these individuals are to be considered American oligarchs, it's worth noting that they are not within the same families, nor do they all support the same causes. Instead, these wealthy people donate to campaigns and causes that help their businesses and promote their ideologies.

The *Washington Post* found that just 10 mega-donor individuals and couples contributed nearly 20% of the $1.1 billion raised by super PACs in 2016. Super PACs are political action committees that can shield the identity of their donors. The top givers included both Democratic and Republican donors.[6]

These backers are well-known on both sides. For example, Charles Koch and his late brother David made their wealth by investing in oil derivatives, and now the Koch family supports conservative politics through the Koch foundations.[7,8] Another example is Harold Hamm, owner of Continental Resources, who opened up the Bakken shale oil fields.[9,10] Continental Resources has used its money to support Republican candidates, PACs, and causes.[11,12]

Comcast lobbyist David Cohen is a millionaire who donates to Democrats. He also successfully lobbied the government for the merger of Comcast and NBC.[13, 14, 15] S. Donald Sussman is a hedge fund manager who supports liberal candidates.[16]

A study reported by researchers from Northwestern and Princeton universities supports claims of an American oligarchy. The study involved reviewing nearly 1,800 federal policies enacted between 1981 and 2002. It found that government policies are substantially influenced by both the economic elite and organized groups representing business interests, while "average citizens and mass-based interest groups have little or no independent influence."[17]

American Disenfranchisement

As a result, many Americans feel disenfranchised or helpless to influence their society. Gallup polls in 2019 consistently found that between 62% and 72% of Americans feel dissatisfied with the way things are going right now.[18] Also, 2018 polls found that only 32% are satisfied with income distribution, though those same polls found that 63% of Americans were satisfied with their opportunity to get ahead in society. However, that's down from the 76% of Americans who felt satisfied with their opportunity to get ahead in 2001.[19]

These attitudes have led to populist protest groups such as the Tea Party and the Occupy Wall Street movements.

This dissatisfaction became a critical force in the 2016 presidential campaign. It created momentum for candidates on both ends of the political spectrum. Bernie Sanders railed against policies that perpetuated income inequality. Donald Trump lumped Republican opponents, Democrats, and powerful corporate lobbyists into the same "swamp" that prevented the federal government from doing the will of the people.

Whether or not President Trump has worked to "drain the swamp" during his time in office is a point of debate.

Is America a Democracy or an Oligarchy?

Endnotes

1. Encyclopedia Britannica. "Oligarchy." Accessed April 29, 2020.
2. World Population Review. "Oligarchy Countries 2020." Accessed April 29, 2020.
3. Encyclopedia Britannica. "Iron Law of Oligarchy." Accessed April 29, 2020.
4. The American Prospect. "What Does Oligarchy Mean?" Accessed April 29, 2020.
5. Pew Research Center. "Trends in US Income and Wealth Inequality." Accessed April 29, 2020.
6. The *Washington Post*. "How 10 Mega-Donors Already Helped Pour a Record $1.1 Billion Into Super Pacs." Accessed March 29, 2020.
7. Securities and Exchange Commission. "Summary of Koch Industries' Industry Facts." Accessed April 29, 2020.
8. Center for Responsive Politics. "Koch Industries." Accessed April 29, 2020.
9. Continental Resources. "Harold G. Hamm." Accessed April 29, 2020.
10. Continental Resources. "Bakken." Accessed April 29, 2020.
11. OpenSecrets.org. "Continental Resources." Accessed April 29, 2020.
12. Federal Election Commission. "Committee Details for Committee ID C00551184." Accessed April 29, 2020.
13. OpenSecrets.org. "Client Profile: Comcast Corp." Accessed April 29, 2020.
14. US House of Representatives Document Repository. "Competition in the Video and Broadband Markets: The Proposed Merger of Comcast and Time Warner Cable," Pages 12-14, 267-318. Accessed April 29, 2020.
15. Comcast. "David L. Cohen, Senior Executive Vice President." Accessed April 29, 2020.
16. OpenSecrets.org. "The Most Generous Megadonors of the 2020 Cycle—So Far." Accessed April 29, 2020.
17. Cambridge Core. "Testing Theories of American Politics: Elites, Interest Groups, and Average Citizens." Accessed April 29, 2020.
18. Gallup. "Satisfaction with the United States." Accessed April 29, 2020.
19. Gallup. "Majority in US Satisfied With Opportunity to Get Ahead." Accessed April 29, 2020.

2

Income Inequality in the United States
Matthew Johnston

Matthew Johnston is professor of macroeconomics and Southeast Asian history at St. Stephen's University in New Brunswick, Canada.

In this viewpoint, the author examines the history of income distribution and associated levels of inequality in the United States from the early twentieth century to the present day. Particular attention is reserved for the impact of fiscal policy and global political dynamics. About 1 percent of Americans receive 22 percent of the nation's total income. New government policies and changes to income tax laws could reduce income inequality and improve many of the social problems that plague the United States, but history tells us the wealthy will likely continue to be favored.

It is not surprising that income inequality has been a major topic in the US presidential race, at least for the Democrats. Near the end of 2013 the *Economist* published an article claiming that out of any highly developed nation in the world the US had the highest after-tax and transfer level of income inequality, with a Gini coefficient of 0.42.

With a host of social ills correlated with high levels of income inequality, it is crucial we figure out how to reduce America's income inequality. Fortunately, history gives us a useful guide to policies that can be implemented to do just that. A brief history of

"A Brief History of Income Inequality in the United States," by Matthew Johnston, Dotdash Publishing Family, June 25, 2019. Reprinted by permission.

income inequality in the US from the beginning of the twentieth century until the present day shows that the nation's level of income inequality is largely affected by government policies concerning taxation and labor.

The Beginning of the Twentieth Century

In 1915, forty years since the US had overtaken the UK as the world's largest economy, a statistician by the name of Willford I. King expressed concern over the fact that approximately 15% of America's income went to the nation's richest 1%. A more recent study by Thomas Piketty and Emmanuel Saez estimates that, in 1913, about 18% of income went to the top 1%.

Perhaps, it is no wonder then that America's current income tax was first introduced in 1913. Being strongly advocated by agrarian and populist parties, the income tax was introduced under the guise of equity, justice, and fairness. One Democrat from Oklahoma, William H. Murray, claimed, "The purpose of this tax is nothing more than to levy a tribute upon that surplus wealth which requires extra expense, and in doing so, it is nothing more than meting out even-handed justice."

While there was a personal tax exemption of $3,000 included in the income tax bill that passed, ensuring that only the wealthiest would be subject to taxation, the new income tax did little to level the playing field between the rich and poor. There was never any intention of it being used to redistribute wealth; instead, it was used to compensate for the lost revenues of reducing excessively high tariffs, of which the rich were the main beneficiaries. Thus, the income tax was more equitable in the sense that the rich were no longer allowed to receive their free lunch but had to start contributing their fair share to government revenues.

The new income tax did little to put a cap on incomes, evidenced by the low top marginal tax rate of 7% on income over $500,000, which in 2013 inflation-adjusted dollars is $11,595,657. Income inequality continued to rise until 1916, the same year in which the top marginal tax rate was raised to 15%. The top rate was changed subsequently in 1917 and 1918 reaching a high of 73% on incomes over $1,000,000.

Interestingly, after reaching a peak in 1916, the top 1% share of income began to drop reaching a low of just under 15% of total income in 1923. After 1923, income inequality began to rise again reaching a new peak in 1928—just before the crash that would usher in the Great Depression—with the richest 1% possessing 19.6% of all income. Not surprisingly, this rise in income inequality also closely mirrors a reduction in top marginal tax rates starting in 1921 with the top rate falling to 25% on income over $100,000 in 1925.

While the relationship between marginal tax rates and income inequality is interesting, it is also worth mentioning that at the beginning of the twentieth century, total union membership in the US stood at about 10% of the labor force. While this number escalated during the First World War, reaching almost 20% by the end of the war, anti-union movements of the 1920s eliminated most of these membership gains.

From the Great Depression to the Great Compression

While the Great Depression served to reduce income inequality, it also decimated total income, leading to mass unemployment and hardship. This left workers without much left to lose, leading to organized pressure for policy reforms. Further, progressive business interests that believed part of the economic crisis and inability to recover was at least partly due to less than optimal aggregate demand as a result of low wages and incomes. These factors combined would provide a fertile climate for the progressive reforms enacted by the New Deal.

With the New Deal providing workers with greater bargaining power, union membership would reach over 33% by 1945, staying above 24% until the early 1970s. During this time, median compensation increased and labor productivity approximately doubled, increasing total prosperity while ensuring that it was being shared more equitably.

Further, during the Great Depression, marginal tax rates were increased numerous times and by 1944, the top marginal tax rate was 94% on all income more than $200,000, which in 2013 inflation-adjusted dollars is $2,609,023. Such a high rate acts as a cap on incomes as it discourages individuals from negotiating additional income above the rate at which the tax would apply and firms from offering such incomes. The top marginal tax rate would remain high for almost four decades, falling to just 70% in 1965, and subsequently to 50% in 1982.

Significantly, during the Great Depression, income inequality came down from its peak in 1929 and was relatively stable with the richest 1% taking approximately 15% of total income between 1930 and 1941. Between 1942 and 1952, the top 1% share of income had dropped to below 10% of total income, stabilizing at around 8% for nearly three decades. This period of income compression has been aptly named the Great Compression.

From the Great Divergence to the Great Recession

The shared prosperity of the decades following World War II would come to an end during the 1970s, a decade characterized by slow growth, high unemployment, and high inflation. This dismal economic situation provided the impetus for new policies that promised to stimulate more economic growth.

Unfortunately, it meant growth would return but the main beneficiaries would be those at the top of the income ladder. Labor unions came under attack in the workplace, courts and in public policy, top marginal tax rates were reduced in an attempt to direct more money towards private investment rather than in the hands of government, and deregulation of corporate and financial institutions were enacted.

In 1978, labor union membership stood at 23.8% and fell to 11.3% in 2011. While the three decades following World War II was an era of shared prosperity, the declining strength of unions has been met with a situation in which labor productivity has doubled since 1973 but median wages have only increased by 4%.

The top marginal tax rate dropped from 70% to 50% in 1982 and then to 38.5% in 1987, and over the past 30 odd years has fluctuated between 28% and 39.6%, which is where it currently sits.

The decline in union membership and reduction of marginal tax rates roughly coincides with increases in income inequality which has come to called the Great Divergence. In 1976, the richest 1% possessed just under 8% of total income but has increased since, reaching a peak of just over 18%—about 23.5% when capital gains are included—in 2007, on the eve of the onset of the Great Recession. These numbers are eerily close to those reached in 1928 that led to the crash that would usher in the Great Depression.

The Bottom Line

History can be a helpful guide to the present. Far from accepting the current economic situation as inevitable, a brief history of income inequality in the US is evidence that government policies can tilt the balance of economic compensation for the rich or the poor. With the last thirty-five years being disproportionately favorable to the wealthy, and the fact that greater income inequality has been correlated with higher levels of crime, stress, mental illness, and some other social ills, it's about time to start leveling the playing field once again.

3

Inequality Is a Threat to Democracy
The Guardian

The Guardian *is a UK-based newspaper founded in 1821. It is owned by the Scott Trust, which was established in 1936 specifically "to secure the financial and editorial independence of the* Guardian *in perpetuity."*

This editorial from the Guardian *argues that privatization and other free market policies have concentrated economic power and produced extreme levels of inequality, and that these conditions represent a threat to the stability of democratic institutions. Democracy does not thrive when a small elite group holds most of the wealth. Instead of isolating themselves, they must use their money and privilege to encourage a thriving society.*

What happens to society where economic power is becoming concentrated in the hands of the few? The present might provide an unsettling answer. A tiny global elite is experiencing a great flourishing; the masses below them are, at varying rates, being left behind. Last week the landmark World Inequality Report, a data-rich project maintained by more than 100 researchers in more than 70 countries, found that the richest 1% reaped 27% of the world's income between 1980 and 2016. The bottom half of humanity, by contrast, got 12%. While the very poorest people have benefited in the last 40 years, it is the extremely rich who've

---

"The Guardian View on the 1%: Democracy or Oligarchy?" Guardian News & Media Ltd, December 17, 2017. Copyright Guardian News & Media Ltd 2020. Reprinted by permission.

emerged as the big winners. China's economic rise has lifted hundreds of millions out of poverty but the wealth share held by the nation's top 1% doubled from 15% to 30%. Such has been the concentration of wealth in India and Russia that inequality not seen since the time of the Raj and the tsar has reappeared. By 2030, the report warns, just 250 people could own 1.5% of all the wealth in the world.

In the west the prevailing ideology of the last 40 years has been of privatisation, deregulation and most recently austerity. This was grounded in rules that served to hold in check the collective power of electorates. The result was higher profits and dividends, lower personal taxes and—for the richest—a higher share of national income. A culture has embedded the perpetual making and lavish expenditure of wealth. However, this came at the expense of almost everyone else: the age of globalisation has seen the pay of lower- and middle-income groups in North America and Europe stagnate. The toxic afterburn of these policies—moulded by domestic choices as much as global pressures—has poisoned politics. Support for anti-establishment parties is now at its highest level since the 1930s. At the same time, mainstream parties have either been radicalised or considerably weakened.

There are legitimate grievances of citizens that need to be addressed. But they have been stoked often by the worst among us. In Brexit Britain, anti-system resentment is being channelled by an extraordinary set of opportunists whose doublespeak claims that watering down workers' rights will lead to an "overtime boom." Donald Trump taps white working-class anger in the United States but is backing a plan to make the country virtually a tax haven for the richest 0.1%, who will face the lowest tax rates since the Gilded Age. If reactionary nationalists are talking about revolution but in fact entrenching a plutocratic status quo, then the same unfortunate trait can be found in progressive globalism. Emmanuel Macron's desire to tax wages more than business income in France is a bad sign that he privileges mobile wealth-creators over immobile workers.

There is nothing inevitable about how much economic liberty the rich are afforded or how long stagnant incomes last. To its credit, Europe shows the way: if the world follows its path, global inequality will decline. The continent is by no means perfect: there should be EU-wide taxes on the richest companies and individuals because they benefit the most from its tariff-free zone. Citizens must recover the idea that politics offers democratic protection, rooted in an egalitarian tradition. In the UK, it is bewildering to see a housebuilding company pay its chief executive £110m when the firm reaped the benefits of a large government subsidy and share prices that bounced back from post-crash lows. Why are ministers not asking for him to publish his tax return to show he will pay £45m back to the Treasury? A laissez-faire approach has for too long subdued democracy and fostered a hyper-exploitative political economy.

The US supreme court justice Louis Brandeis once correctly observed: "We may have democracy, or we may have wealth concentrated in the hands of a few, but we can't have both." Politicians need to make the case for a more equitable settlement: advocating more progressive taxes and a global financial register to stop wealth being shielded in offshore havens. Government spending on health, education and wellbeing is required for the meaningful exercise of citizenship. The rich must share the burden of common challenges—not just sail away in their tax-haven-registered yachts. The mutinous mood among voters will only deepen when they begin paying carbon taxes, and the rich don't even pay taxes. Contemporary life rests on a fragile consensus that governance works because people believe it does. This faith rests on the rich pulling their weight. Which is why they should.

4

Democracy Doesn't Guarantee Economic Liberty

Arthur Foulkes

Arthur Foulkes is an Indiana-based journalist whose work focuses on capitalism, business, and economic policy.

In this viewpoint written before the financial crisis of 2007–2008 and the ensuing Great Recession, Arthur Foulkes argues that a system with primarily capitalist values guarantees economic freedom more effectively than a system with primarily democratic values. Capitalism is predicated on the limitation of government interference and, unlike democracy, is the only path through which to attain true liberty.

I recently heard a prominent American politician tell how a "chill" went up his spine when he heard someone question the importance of democracy. How could anyone doubt the value of democracy? he wondered. Fortunately, he said, he soon realized that by "democracy" his (European) interlocutor really meant "capitalism." Whew, he thought, that's all right, then. But is democracy really more important than capitalism?

One immediate problem we face discussing democracy and capitalism is that both terms have different meanings for different people. For some people "capitalism" is synonymous with

"Capitalism and Democracy," by Arthur Foulkes, Foundation for Economic Education, November 1, 2006. https://fee.org/articles/capitalism-and-democracy/. Licensed under Creative Commons Attribution 4.0 International.

"corporatism" or "crony capitalism," which combines nominally private enterprises with a highly interventionist political system—indeed, something like the US system today. Likewise, "democracy" for some is synonymous with social and economic equality. For them, no democracy can exist when some people live in poverty, some cannot read, and others live in mansions or attend Ivy League schools.

For my purposes, however, democracy will be defined simply as "the people rule," or, more specifically, "majority rule." While it's true that almost everyone would agree that democracy also requires certain guaranteed freedoms, such as freedom of the press, freedom of speech, and the right of habeas corpus, even these freedoms are subject to limitations when public opinion permits—as any number of examples from periods of crisis in US history can demonstrate.

Capitalism, on the other hand, will here refer to a free-market economy with guaranteed property rights—a laissez-faire society. Indeed, a free market is simply one in which the unhampered exchange of property titles can take place. Thus in a truly capitalist society, government's role would be strictly limited to protecting property rights (including the right to our bodies) since virtually any other government activity would almost certainly involve the violation of those rights. Thus by this definition, the economic system capitalism necessarily implies a (classical) liberal political system.

Democracy, however, makes no promises regarding the size and scope of government. Indeed, it could be argued that democracy is inherently hostile to limited government since many citizens in a democracy (including many so-called "capitalists") soon find they can successfully lobby government officials for subsidies, trade protection, and other legal privileges. Likewise, elected officials soon learn it is in their interest to strategically grant economic favors for their own political and electoral needs. As economist Randall G. Holcombe noted in "Liberty and Democracy as Economic Systems" (*Independent Review*), "There are inherent tensions between democracy and a free-market economy that make it difficult to maintain a stable system. In particular, the ascendancy of democracy threatens the survival of the free-market economy, which was built on a foundation of liberty. ... The evolution of democracy has come at the expense of liberty."

Or as economist John Wenders wrote in the *Freeman*: "Democracy evolves into kleptocracy."

The original design for the American government was one that attempted to combine limited democracy with limited government. But it didn't take long for this ideal to begin to dissolve.

One of the first blows came when George Washington was president, during a debate over the meaning of the Constitution's Necessary and Proper clause. Washington and a congressional majority planted some of the first seeds of big government when they accepted the argument of Treasury Secretary Alexander Hamilton, who contended that the clause (taken along with the fact that the Tenth Amendment's reservation of state powers failed to include the word "expressly") gave the federal government powers beyond those specified in Article I, Section 8. Hamilton's vision won the day despite opposition from Thomas Jefferson and the Constitution's principal author, James Madison, who feared that "such a broad interpretation of the 'necessary and proper clause' would allow the federal government a reach far beyond the intentions of the Constitution's framers." Within 20 years the Supreme Court would endorse Hamilton 's view.

Despite this and some other notable setbacks in the nineteenth century, for most of the first hundred years of American history, Congress, the president, and the courts took fairly seriously the idea that the federal government should be limited and that the Tenth Amendment—stating that any powers not delegated to the national government by the Constitution are reserved to the states or to the people—still had some meaning. The real damage came in the twentieth century. As the Cato Institute's Roger Pilon told a Senate subcommittee in 2005:

> *The great constitutional change took place in 1937 and 1938, during the New Deal, all without benefit of constitutional*

amendment; but the seeds for the change had been sown well before that, during the Progressive Era. ...

Search the Constitution as you will, you will find no authority for Congress to appropriate and spend federal funds on education, agriculture, disaster relief, retirement programs, housing, health care, day care, the arts, public broadcasting—this list is endless. ... [T]he Constitution says, in effect, that everything that is not authorized—to the government . . . is forbidden. [The] Progressives turned that on its head: Everything that is not forbidden is authorized.

How We Got Here

I recently asked a class of mine to speculate just how the United States moved from having a national government that Madison described as having powers that were "few and defined" to one that doesn't hesitate to spend billions of tax dollars on everything from space exploration to "pro-marriage programs." None of my students could say, but it is interesting to note that a significant shift away from liberty and toward interventionism came at the behest of so-called "capitalist entrepreneurs" during the Progressive period.

Conventional wisdom still holds that the Progressive era was in large part a response to a growing monopolization and concentration of economic power in fewer and fewer hands around the start of the twentieth century. The exact opposite is more the case. Unrelenting competition and market uncertainties led large business interests to lobby government for regulations designed to stifle their competitors. As Marxist historian Gabriel Kolko noted in his classic, *The Triumph of Conservatism*:

> *Competition was unacceptable to many key business and financial interests. ... As new competitors sprang up, and as economic power was diffused throughout an expanding nation, it became apparent to many important businessmen that only the national government could rationalize the economy. ... Ironically, contrary to the consensus of historians, it was not the existence of monopoly that caused the federal government to intervene in the economy, but lack of it.*

Yet this increase in government power did not take place in a vacuum; public opinion had to allow it. As Robert Higgs noted in his important book *Crisis and Leviathan*, "Ideology, which some refer to more vaguely as 'public opinion,' must have played an important part, at least a decisive permissive role. ... If people generally had opposed Big Government on principle, free markets could scarcely have been abandoned as they have been during the past seventy years."

A related view takes the importance of ideology a step further by suggesting that the Constitution never really limited the government at all. Former FEE president Donald Boudreaux writes, "[T]he constitution is the dominant ideology within us—an ideology that determines what we permit each other to do, as well as what we permit government to do. No words on parchment ... will ever override the prevailing belief system of the people who form a polity."

In other words, ideas count more than articles and amendments. As the American people have come to expect more from their government, the size of that government has grown and their "constitutional tolerance" has grown with it, all but washing away America's classical-liberal roots. Modern political leaders have found this to their advantage. As government expands, their political power and influence expand with it. Fewer and fewer aspects of life are left to private individuals, while more and more decisions are made by government officials. This may be called "democracy," but it is clearly the substituting of the public and the political for the private and the voluntary—that is, the coercive for the peaceful.

As noted, many contemporary critics of capitalism believe a "true" democracy means a powerful state role in promoting economic equality, "fair" labor conditions, "socially responsible" economic growth, and so on. Their plans always involve greater restrictions on private property rights and other personal freedoms. And while they believe they are promoting equality, their vision necessarily implies a tremendous inequality of political power. As economist Peter Bauer once noted, "The successful pursuit of the unholy grail of economic equality would exchange the promised reduction or removal of differences in income and wealth for much greater actual inequality of power between rulers and subjects."

"Fat Cats" for Capitalism?

To promote their case, many of capitalism's critics assert that only corporate "fat cats" benefit from economic freedom. But as Madsen Pirie noted in his essay "Nine Lies about Capitalism," "If capitalism really served the interests of businessmen, then more of them would be in favor of it." As noted, some of the most damaging and powerful opponents of truly free markets have been, and continue to be, business leaders. This is unsurprising. When markets are free, businessmen are the servants of consumers and those who fail to satisfy consumers are ultimately doomed. Yet it is this uncertainty that leads to greater overall prosperity. The profit (and loss) system, so decried by anti-capitalists, is the springboard for constant innovation and greater productivity—in other words, improved living standards for everyone.

Democracy and liberty can coexist only if public opinion favors private property rights and individual freedom over coercion. Capitalism, not democracy, implies just this sort of liberty; democracy only implies that government is directed by mass opinion. Today, because liberty is often confused with the "right to vote," true liberty is more and more threatened by expanded and expanding "democracy." Yet, as John Wenders has noted (in words I would love to see emblazoned on a monument somewhere in Washington), "Freedom is not measured by the ability to vote. It is measured by the breadth of those things on which we do not vote."

To limit the reach of government in a democratic system may indeed be limiting the reach of democracy itself. Yet this is no bad thing if by limiting the reach of democracy we are in turn securing liberty.

5

Inequality Has Resulted in a Populist Surge

Michael Sandel

Michael Sandel is professor of government theory at Harvard University Law School. He is the author of numerous influential works on political philosophy, including Liberalism and the Limits of Justice *and* Democracy's Discontent: America in Search of a Public Philosophy.

In this viewpoint, the influential political philosopher Michael Sandel examines a number of contemporary trends that represent major threats to the future of democracy, including surging populism across the globe in the Trump era. This populism has been growing for decades as an angry response to economic policies that, whether they are intended to or not, favor elites rather than middle class and working-class Americans.

These are dangerous times for democracy. Russia, Turkey, Hungary, Poland, and other places that once offered democratic hope are now, in varying degrees, falling into authoritarianism. Democracy is also in trouble in sturdier places.

In the United States, Donald Trump poses the greatest threat to the American constitutional order since Richard Nixon. And yet, despite the floundering first year and a half of Trump's presidency, the opposition has yet to find its voice.

"Populism, Trump, and the Future of Democracy," by Michael Sandel, Institute for New Economic Thinking, March 15, 2019. Reprinted by permission.

One might think that Trump's inflammatory tweets, erratic behavior, and persistent disregard for democratic norms would offer the opposition an easy target. But it has not worked out this way. For those who would mount a politics of resistance, the outrage Trump provokes has been less energizing than paralyzing.

There are two reasons for the opposition's paralysis. One is the investigation by special counsel Robert Mueller into the Trump campaign's possible collusion with Russia. The hope that Mueller's findings will lead to the impeachment of Trump is wishful thinking that distracts Democrats from asking hard questions about why voters have rejected them at both the federal and state level.

A second source of paralysis lies in the chaos Trump creates. His steady stream of provocations has a disorienting effect on critics, who struggle to discriminate between the more consequential affronts to democracy and passing distractions.

The Italian writer Italo Calvino once wrote, "I spent the first twenty years of my life with Mussolini's face always in view." Trump too is always in view, thanks partly to his tweets and partly to the insatiable appetite of television news to cover his every outrageous antic.

An Economy of Outrage

Moral outrage can be politically energizing, but only if it is channeled and guided by political judgment. What the opposition to Trump needs now is an economy of outrage, disciplined by the priorities of an affirmative political project.

What might such a project look like? To answer this question, we must begin by facing up to the complacencies of establishment political thinking that opened the way to Trump in the US and to right-wing populism in Britain and Europe.

The hard reality is that Donald Trump was elected by tapping a wellspring of anxieties, frustrations, and legitimate grievances to which the mainstream parties have no compelling answer.

This means that, for those worried about Trump, and about populism, it is not enough to mobilize a politics of protest and resistance; it is also necessary to engage in a politics of persuasion. Such a politics must begin by understanding the discontent that is roiling politics in the US and in democracies around the world. It is not enough to mobilize a politics of protest and resistance; it is also necessary to engage in a politics of persuasion.

The Failure of Technocratic Liberalism

Like the triumph of Brexit in the UK, the election of Trump was an angry verdict on decades of rising inequality and a version of globalization that benefits those at the top but leaves ordinary people feeling disempowered. It was also a rebuke for a technocratic approach to politics that is tone deaf to the resentments of people who feel the economy and the culture have left them behind.

Some denounce the upsurge of populism as little more than a racist, xenophobic reaction against immigrants and multiculturalism. Others see it mainly in economic terms, as a protest against the job losses brought about by global trade and new technologies.

But it is a mistake to see only the bigotry in populist protest, or to view it only as an economic complaint. To do so misses the fact that the upheavals we are witnessing are a political response to a political failure of historic proportions. The upheavals we are witnessing are a political response to a political failure of historic proportions.

The right wing populism ascendant today is a symptom of the failure of progressive politics. The Democratic Party has become a party of a technocratic liberalism more congenial to the professional classes than to the blue collar and middle class voters who once constituted its base. A similar predicament afflicted Britain's Labour Party and led, following its defeat in the last general election, to the surprising election of anti-establishment figure Jeremy Corbyn as party leader.

The roots of the predicament go back to the 1980s. Ronald Reagan and Margaret Thatcher had argued that government was the problem and that markets were the solution. When they passed from the political scene, the center-left politicians who succeeded them—Bill Clinton in the US, Tony Blair in Britain, Gerhard Schroeder in Germany—moderated but consolidated the market faith. They softened the harsh edges of unfettered markets, but did not challenge the central premise of the Reagan-Thatcher era—that market mechanisms are the primary instruments for achieving the public good. In line with this faith, they embraced a market-driven version of globalization and welcomed the growing financialization of the economy.

In the 1990s, the Clinton administration joined with Republicans in promoting global trade agreements and deregulating the financial industry. The benefits of these policies flowed mostly to those at the top, but Democrats did little to address the deepening inequality and the growing power of money in politics. Having strayed from its traditional mission of taming capitalism and holding economic power to democratic account, liberalism lost its capacity to inspire. Having strayed from its traditional mission of taming capitalism and holding economic power to democratic account, liberalism lost its capacity to inspire.

All that seemed to change when Barack Obama appeared on the political scene. In his 2008 presidential campaign, he offered a stirring alternative to the managerial, technocratic language that had come to characterize liberal public discourse. He showed that progressive politics could speak a language of moral and spiritual purpose.

But the moral energy and civic idealism he inspired as a candidate did not carry over into his presidency. Assuming office in the midst of the financial crisis, he appointed economic advisors who had promoted financial deregulation during the Clinton years. With their encouragement, he bailed out the banks on terms that did not hold them to account for the behavior that led to the crisis and offered little help for ordinary citizens who had lost their homes.

His moral voice muted, Obama placated rather than articulated the seething public anger toward Wall Street. Lingering anger over the bailout cast a shadow over the Obama presidency and would ultimately fuel a mood of populist protest that reached across the political spectrum—on the left, the Occupy movement and the candidacy of Bernie Sanders, on the right, the Tea Party movement and the election of Trump. His moral voice muted, Obama placated rather than articulated the seething public anger toward Wall Street.

The populist uprising in the US, Britain, and Europe is a backlash against elites of the mainstream parties, but its most conspicuous causalities have been liberal and center-left political parties—the Democratic Party in the US, the Labour Party in Britain, the Social Democratic Party (SPD) in Germany, whose share of the vote reached a historic low in the last Federal election, Italy's Democratic Party, whose vote share dropped to less than 20 per cent, and the Socialist Party in France, whose presidential nominee won only six per cent of the vote in the first round of last year's election.

Rethinking Progressive Politics

Before they can hope to win back public support, progressive parties must rethink their mission and purpose. To do so, they should learn from the populist protest that has displaced them—not by replicating its xenophobia and strident nationalism, but by taking seriously the legitimate grievances with which these ugly sentiments are entangled. Such rethinking should begin with the recognition that these grievances are not only economic but also moral and cultural; they are not only about wages and jobs but also about social esteem.

Here are four themes that progressive parties need to grapple with if they hope to address the anger and resentments that roil politics today: income inequality; meritocratic hubris; the dignity of work; patriotism and national community:

Income Inequality

The standard response to inequality is to call for greater equality of opportunity—retraining workers whose jobs have disappeared due to globalization and technology; improving access to higher education; removing barriers of race, ethnicity, and gender. It is summed up in the slogan that those who work hard and play by the rules should be able to rise as far as their talents will take them.

But this slogan now rings hollow. In today's economy, it is not easy to rise. This is a special problem for the US, which prides itself on upward mobility. Americans have traditionally worried less than Europeans about inequality, believing that, whatever one's starting point in life, it is possible, with hard work, to rise from rags to riches. But today, this belief is in doubt. Americans born to poor parents tend to stay poor as adults. Of those born in the bottom fifth of the income scale, 43 per cent will remain there, and only four per cent will make it to the top fifth. It is easier to rise from poverty in Canada, Germany, Sweden, and other European countries than it is in the US.

This may explain why the rhetoric of opportunity fails to inspire as it once did. Progressives should reconsider the assumption that mobility can compensate for inequality. They should reckon directly with inequalities of power and wealth, rather than rest content with the project of helping people scramble up a ladder whose rungs grow further and further apart.

Meritocratic Hubris

But the problem runs deeper. The relentless emphasis on creating a fair meritocracy, in which social positions reflect effort and talent, has a corrosive effect on the way we interpret our success (or the lack of it). The notion that the system rewards talent and hard work encourages the winners to consider their success their own doing, a measure of their virtue—and to look down upon those less fortunate than themselves.

Those who lose out may complain that the system is rigged, that the winners have cheated and manipulated their way to the top. Or they may harbor the demoralizing thought that their failure is their own doing, that they simply lack the talent and drive to succeed.

When these sentiments coexist, as invariably they do, they make for a volatile brew of anger and resentment against elites that fuels populist protest. Though himself a billionaire, Donald Trump understands and exploits this resentment. Unlike Barack Obama and Hillary Clinton, who spoke constantly of "opportunity," Trump scarcely mentions the word. Instead, he offers blunt talk of winners and losers.

Liberals and progressives have so valorized a college degree—both as an avenue for advancement and as the basis for social esteem—that they have difficulty understanding the hubris a meritocracy can generate, and the harsh judgment it imposes on those who have not gone to college. Such attitudes are at the heart of the populist backlash and Trump's victory.

One of the deepest political divides in American politics today is between those with and those without a college degree. To heal this divide, Democrats need to understand the attitudes toward merit and work it reflects.

The Dignity of Work

The loss of jobs to technology and outsourcing has coincided with a sense that society accords less respect to the kind of work the working class does. As economic activity has shifted from making things to managing money, as society has lavished outsized rewards on hedge fund managers and Wall Street bankers, the esteem accorded work in the traditional sense has become fragile and uncertain.

New technologies may further erode the dignity of work. Some Silicon Valley visionaries anticipate a time when robots and artificial intelligence will render many of today's jobs obsolete. To ease the way for such a future, they propose paying everyone a basic income. What was once justified as a safety net for all citizens is now offered as a way to soften the transition to a world without work. Whether such a world is a prospect to welcome or to resist is a question that will be central to politics in the coming years. To think it through, political parties will have to grapple with the meaning of work and its place in a good life.

Patriotism and National Community

Free trade agreements and immigration are the most potent flashpoints of populist fury. On one level, these are economic issues. Opponents argue that free trade agreements and immigration threaten local jobs and wages, while proponents reply that they help the economy in the long run. But the passion these issues evoke suggests something more is at stake.

Workers who believe their country cares more for cheap goods and cheap labor than for the job prospects of its own people feel betrayed. This sense of betrayal often finds ugly, intolerant expression—a hatred of immigrants, a strident nationalism that vilifies Muslims and other "outsiders," a rhetoric of "taking back our country."

Liberals reply by condemning the hateful rhetoric and insisting on the virtues of mutual respect and multicultural understanding. But this principled response, valid though it is, fails to address an important set of questions implicit in the populist complaint. What is the moral significance, if any, of national borders? Do we owe more to our fellow citizens than we owe citizens of other countries? In a global age, should we cultivate national identities or aspire to a cosmopolitan ethic of universal human concern?

These questions may seem daunting, a far cry from the small things we discuss in politics these days. But the populist uprising highlights the need to rejuvenate democratic public discourse, to address the big questions people care about, including moral and cultural questions.

Revitalizing Public Discourse

Any attempt to address such questions, to reimagine the terms of democratic public discourse, faces a powerful obstacle. It requires that we rethink a central premise of contemporary liberalism. It requires that we question the idea that the way to a tolerant society is to avoid engaging in substantive moral argument in politics.

This principle of avoidance—this insistence that citizens leave their moral and spiritual convictions outside when they enter the public square—is a powerful temptation. It seems to avoid the danger that the majority may impose its values on the minority. It seems to prevent the possibility that a morally overheated politics will lead to wars of religion. It seems to offer a secure basis for mutual respect.

But this strategy of avoidance, this insistence on liberal neutrality, is a mistake. It ill-equips us to address the moral and cultural issues that animate the populist revolt. For how is it possible to discuss the meaning of work and its role in a good life without debating competing conceptions of the good life? How is it possible to think through the proper relation of national and global identities without asking about the virtues such identities express, and the claims they make upon us?

Liberal neutrality flattens questions of meaning, identity, and purpose into questions of fairness. It therefore misses the anger and resentment that animate the populist revolt; it lacks the moral and rhetorical and sympathetic resources to understand the cultural estrangement, even humiliation, that many working class and middle class voters feel; and it ignores the meritocratic hubris of elites. Donald Trump is keenly alive to the politics of humiliation.

From the standpoint of economic fairness, his populism is fake, a kind of plutocratic populism. His health plan would have cut health care for many of his working class supporters to fund massive tax cuts for the wealthy. But to focus solely on this hypocrisy misses the point.

When he withdrew the US from the Paris climate change agreement, Trump argued, implausibly, that he was doing so to protect American jobs. But the real point of his decision, its political rationale, was contained in this seemingly stray remark: "We don't want other countries and other leaders to laugh at us anymore."

Liberating the US from the supposed burdens of the climate change agreement was not really about jobs or about global warming. It was, in Trump's political imagination, about averting humiliation. This resonates with Trump voters, even those who care about climate change.

For those left behind by three decades of market-driven globalization, the problem is not only wage stagnation and the loss of jobs; it is also the loss of social esteem. It is not only about unfairness; it is also about humiliation. It is not only about unfairness; it is also about humiliation.

Mainstream liberal and social democratic politicians miss this dimension of politics. They think the problem with globalization is simply a matter of distributive justice; those who have gained from global trade, new technologies, and the financialization of the economy have not adequately compensated those who have lost out.

But this misunderstands the populist complaint. It also reflects a defect in the public philosophy of contemporary liberalism. Many liberals distinguish between neo-liberalism (or laissez-faire, free market thinking) and the liberalism that finds expression in what philosophers call "liberal public reason." The first is an economic doctrine, whereas the second is a principle of political morality that insists government should be neutral toward competing conceptions of the good life.

Notwithstanding this distinction, there is a philosophical affinity between the neo-liberal faith in market reasoning and the principle of liberal neutrality. Market reasoning is appealing because it seems to offer a way to resolve contested public questions without engaging in contentious debates about how goods are properly valued. When two people make a deal, they decide for themselves what value to place on the goods they exchange.

Similarly, liberal neutrality is appealing because it seems to offer a way of defining and justifying rights without presupposing any particular conception of the good. But the neutrality is spurious in both cases. Markets are not morally neutral instruments for defining the common good. And liberal public reason is not a morally neutral way of arriving at principles of justice. Markets are not morally neutral instruments for defining the common good. And liberal public reason is not a morally neutral way of arriving at principles of justice.

Conducting our public discourse as if it were possible to outsource moral judgment to markets, or to procedures of liberal public reason, has created an empty, impoverished public discourse, a vacuum of public meaning. Such empty public spaces are invariably filled by narrow, intolerant, authoritarian alternatives—whether in the form of religious fundamentalism or strident nationalism.

That is what we are witnessing today. Three decades of market-driven globalization and technocratic liberalism have hollowed out democratic public discourse, disempowered ordinary citizens, and prompted a populist backlash that seeks to cloth the naked public square with an intolerant, vengeful nationalism.

A Vacuum of Public Meaning

To reinvigorate democratic politics, we need to find our way to a morally more robust public discourse, one that honors pluralism by engaging with our moral disagreements, rather than avoiding them.

Disentangling the intolerant aspects of populist protest from its legitimate grievances is no easy matter. But it is important to try. Understanding these grievances and creating a politics that can respond to them is the most pressing political challenge of our time.

The Politics of Progressive Reform in the United States

Daniel T. Rodgers

Daniel T. Rodgers is professor emeritus of history at Princeton University. He is the author of numerous books, including Atlantic Crossings: Social Politics in a Progressive Age *(2000) and* Age of Fracture *(2011), for which he received the Bancroft Prize.*

In this viewpoint, the historian Daniel T. Rodgers looks at the politics of class, income, and economics in the United States during the progressive era. This era in American history saw a number of policies designed and implemented specifically to address the economic conditions of the late nineteenth century, which were widely perceived as oligarchic.

We should not accept social life as it has "trickled down to us," the young journalist Walter Lippmann wrote soon after the twentieth century began. "We have to deal with it deliberately, devise its social organization, . . . educate and control it." The ambition to harness and organize the energies of modern life of which Lippmann spoke cut through American economy, politics, and society in many different, sometimes contradictory ways between 1900 and 1929, but it left virtually none of its major institutions unchanged. The modern business corporation, modern politics, the modern presidency, a modern vision of the

---

"The Progressive Era to the New Era, 1900–1929," by Daniel T. Rodgers, The Gilder Lehrman Institute of American History. Reprinted by permission.

international order, and modern consumer capitalism were all born in these years.

More than in most eras, Americans in the first years of the twentieth century felt the newness of their place in history. Looking back on the late nineteenth century, they stressed its chaos: the boom-and-bust cycles of the economy, the violent and exploitative aspects of its economy and social life, the gulf between its ostentatious new wealth and the lot of its urban poor and hard-pressed farmers, and the inefficiency of American politics in a world of great nations.

A Revolution in Organization

The pioneers in the reorganization of social life on more deliberate and systematic lines were the architects of the modern business corporation. In the aftermath of the 1890s depression, they undertook to supplant the unstable partnership and credit systems of the past with the forms of the modern corporation: broadly capitalized, more intensely managed, and national in scope and market. The reorganization of Andrew Carnegie's iron and steel empire by the J. P. Morgan banking house into the mammoth US Steel Corporation in 1901 was a sign of the trends to come. By the 1920s, corporate giants in production, communications, finance, life insurance, and entertainment dominated the economy; the two hundred largest corporations in 1929 owned nearly half the nation's total corporate wealth.

The new scale of economic enterprise demanded much more systematic organization. On the shop and office floor the systematization of work routines was intense, from the elaborate organization of clerical labor at Metropolitan Life to the subdivision of automobile making at Ford in 1913 into tasks that workers could repeat over and over as an assembly line dragged their work past them. In the showcases of "welfare capitalism," a new cadre of personnel managers undertook to smooth out the radically unstable hiring and firing practices of the past, creating seniority systems and benefits for stable employees. By the 1920s the corporate elite was heralding a "new era" for capitalism, freed of the cyclical instabilities of the past. Its watchwords now were efficiency, permanence, welfare, and service.

With similar ambition to escape the turbulence of late nineteenth-century economy and society, progressive reformers undertook to expand the capacities of governments to deal with the worst effects of barely regulated capitalism. Their projects met far more resistance than those of the corporate managers. But between 1900 and 1929 they succeeded in bringing most of the characteristics of the modern administrative state into being. More professionalized corps of state factory inspectors endeavored to safeguard workers from dangerous working conditions, physically exhausting hours, and industrial diseases. Public utility commissions endeavored to pull the pricing of railroad shipping, streetcar fares, and city gas and water supplies out of the turmoil of politics and put them in the hands of expert-staffed commissions charged with setting fair terms of service and fair return on capital. New zoning boards, city planning commissions, and public health bureaus sprang into being to try to bring more conscious public order out of chaotic land markets, slum housing, poisoned food, polluted water supplies, and contagious diseases.

Progressive Politics

The energy of the new progressive politics was most intense at the state and local levels where civic reform associations of all sorts sprang up to thrust the new economic and social issues into politics. Women's leagues, labor federations, businessmen's good government lobbies, social welfare associations, and investigative journalists led the way, borrowing on each other's techniques and successes.

Despite the more sharply defined constitutional limitations on federal power in this period, visions of more active government filtered up into national politics as well. Theodore Roosevelt set the mold for a much more active, issue-driven presidency than any since the Civil War. Roosevelt brought an anti-trust rhetoric and a powerful interest in environmental conservation into politics. In the national railroad strike of 1894, President Cleveland had dispatched federal troops to break the strike; now in the national coal strike of 1902, Roosevelt offered the White House as a venue for mediation. Pushed by its farm and labor constituencies, the Democratic Party, too, moved toward more active and effective governance. The era's impetus for the creation of a more centralized banking system to stabilize the nation's credit system had come first from elite bankers. Woodrow Wilson and the Democratic Congress incorporated their plan for a central bank into the Federal Reserve Act of 1913, sliding a publicly appointed board of governors over the bankers' plan for self-regulation. Congress took its first steps toward nation-wide child labor restriction, though the Supreme Court struck down the act on a narrow reading of the Constitution's "commerce clause."

The relationship of these progressive reforms to democracy was complex. To break what they saw as the corrupt alliance between business wealth and political party bosses, progressive reformers succeeded in moving the election of US Senators from the state legislatures to the general electorate and, in some states, instituting new systems of popular referenda, initiative, and recall. They championed votes for women, bringing the last states holding out against women's suffrage into line in the Nineteenth Amendment in 1920. But they also tightened up voting registration systems to curb immigrant voters, and they acquiesced in disfranchisement measures to strike African Americans off the voting rolls that had swept through southern states between 1890 and 1908.

Immigration

The immigrant-filled cities were a focal point for the progressives' mixed feelings about mass democracy. Between 1900 and the outbreak of war in Europe in 1914, more than thirteen million immigrants arrived in the United States, pouring into industrial cities largely from the rural regions of central and southern Europe. The new economy, in which six out of every ten industrial workers in 1914 was born abroad, was built on their cheap labor. Out of this new urban working class sprang not only new forms of poverty and overcrowded, tenement living but also powerful political machines, vigorous labor unions, and a socialist party that on the eve of the First World War rivaled any outside of Germany. Middle-class progressives sometimes took the urban masses as political allies. More often, however, the progressives saw the urban poor as objects of social concerns: as populations to be assimilated, improved, and protected from the employers, landlords, and political bosses who exploited them. Progressives inclined less toward talk of class justice than toward faith in a unitary public good; they thought less in terms of protected rights than of mediation and efficient management. They may have placed too much trust in experts, science, and the idea of the common good, but they brought into being the capacities of the modern state to push back against accidents of social fate and the excesses of private capital.

The International Stage

In all these state-building endeavors, early twentieth-century Americans moved in step with their counterparts in other industrial nations. That meant increasing the capacity of the nation to project its interests more forcefully abroad. In the Philippines, seized as a collateral asset in the war to free Cuba from Spanish rule in 1898, a commission led by William Howard Taft undertook to establish an American-style model of imperial governance. In Latin America, where American economic interests were about to eclipse Britain's, US muscle flexing became routine. On a dozen different occasions between 1906 and 1929, US administrations dispatched troops to Mexico and the Caribbean to seize customs houses, reorganize finances, or attempt to control the outcome of an internal revolution.

The outbreak of war in Europe in 1914 brought these state-building ambitions to a peak. Once the Wilson administration's efforts to trade neutrally with all the belligerents collapsed in

1917, the administration entered the war determined to turn the nation into an efficient social machine for its promotion. Manpower was recruited through a wartime draft. Funds were raised through income tax levies and a public crusade for war bond sales, orchestrated with the best techniques that advertisers and psychological experts could muster. The nation's railroads were temporarily nationalized to coordinate transportation; farmers were organized for war production; the War Industries Board undertook to coordinate industrial production; labor representation rights were granted to boost production and morale; and social workers and psychologists undertook to sort out and ease the transition into war for the almost three million new military recruits. It was only thirteen months between the arrival of US troops in France in October 1917 and the Armistice, but the war gave Americans a model for the efficient mobilization of resources in a common cause that early New Dealers, in particular, would remember.

The First World War gave Americans their first vision of a more effectively managed international order as well. The idea of reorganizing the world for the more efficient management of international disputes had many sources in this period. "Wilsonianism," as it has come to be called, was not uniquely Woodrow Wilson's idea, though he pushed more strongly for it than any of the other great power leaders who met at the peace conference at Versailles in 1919. When the Senate failed to muster the two-thirds necessary to ratify US entry in the new League of Nations, the defeat came as a major blow to progressives. But the application of the label "isolationist" to the period disguises the heightened role that the United States actually played in the organization of international affairs in the 1920s. The nation cooperated with the other great powers in the era's arms-limitation agreements. American banker Charles Dawes won the Nobel Peace Prize in 1925 for engineering a more sustainable international plan for German war reparations payments, soon further eased by the US government's orchestration of new loans to German borrowers. Although the United States was not a participant in the new World Court created under the terms of the peace treaty, an American jurist served on its panel of eleven judges.

Postwar America

Domestically, the break between the prewar and postwar years seemed much sharper than on the international stage. The year 1919, in which the war economic machine ground suddenly to a halt, was one of the most volatile years of the twentieth century. Demobilization unloosed a wave of labor strikes unprecedented in their scale and the radical character of their demands. Workers tried to expand their wartime gains against employers who were determined to drive back unions and reassert management's prerogatives of control. Fearful of revolution abroad and at home, the Justice Department rounded up and deported hundreds of aliens whom it judged, without trial, to be radical and disloyal. Violence erupted along race lines as white mobs in more than twenty cities poured into African American neighborhoods to attack homes and persons. A new Ku Klux Klan emerged in both the North and South with the goal of intimidating not only blacks but also Catholics, immigrants, and radicals. In the aftermath of 1919's turmoil, Warren G. Harding, a Republican presidential candidate committed to returning the nation to "normalcy," swept the election in a landslide. Vice President Calvin Coolidge succeeded Harding after his death in 1923.

Still, many of the managerial ambitions of the earlier years survived into the "new era." Coolidge, who retained the presidency in 1924, was no friend of energetic government, but his commerce secretary and successor, the engineer Herbert Hoover, held much more ambitious ideas of the role of government in promoting business and public ends than he is generally credited with. The massive Hoover Dam public works project was a product of the Coolidge and Hoover administrations; the most important Depression-era agency for financial restabilization, the Reconstruction Finance Administration, began as a Hoover initiative. The drive to prohibit the production and sale of alcohol for consumption undertaken in 1919 and the shuttering of the borders to new European immigration in 1921 were driven in part by moral conservatives' recoil against the mores of the urban, immigrant city. But there were progressives who saw in both measures the promise of a better-organized society, deliberately managing its population movements and curbing the wasteful effects of drunkenness on labor efficiency and on abused wives and children.

The changes that marked the 1900–1929 period were very unevenly spread across the nation's regions and peoples. Southern leaders were not immune to progressive political ambitions. Southern farmers lobbied hard for federal credit systems to supplement private lenders in the cash-strapped South. They turned the system of federally supported agriculture extension agents into a far-flung network of scientific advice, crop marketing assistance, and lobbying help in Congress. But southern progressive reform had its limits. Efforts to enfranchise women, or effectively ban the employment of twelve- and thirteen-year-old children in the textile mills, or enact national anti-lynching legislation met with major resistance. Although there were islands of exception, the South was visibly poorer than the rest of country, much less urbanized, farther from the new consumer society being built elsewhere, and intractably committed to cotton, low-wage labor, and management of its own racial matters.

The most striking change in the South was the massive wartime exodus to the North of African Americans, breaking the ties that had bound most former slaves to agricultural poverty and tenancy since the end of the Civil War. Animosity toward African Americans did not change in the North in this period, where racial pseudo-science flourished in both elite and popular forms, but the labor shortages of the First World War shattered northern employers' bans against African American workers, and the strenuous efforts of southern landlords to keep black labor from fleeing north were not enough to blunt the effects. Almost a half million African Americans fled between 1914 and 1920. Most were rural folk for whom the sharply defined housing ghettoes and racially segregated labor markets of the urban North still seemed a major step up from sharecropping and the codes of southern racial subordination. They were joined by aspiring poets, entrepreneurs, jazz musicians, and rights advocates who helped to make Chicago's South Side and New York City's Harlem magnets for a newly self-conscious, urban, and assertive black politics and culture. New racially segregated labor patterns changed the American Southwest as well, as expanding jobs in the farms, mines, and railroads drew hundreds of thousands of workers across the border with Mexico.

Women experienced the era's changes in more complex ways than men. Northern middle-class women had played a defining role in advancing many of the progressive social reforms of the day. Even before they gained the vote, they had established themselves as important politics actors. Working out from woman-dominated social spaces in the settlement houses, women's clubs and colleges, the social-gospel churches, and the social work professions, they undertook to demonstrate women's higher moral sensibilities and their greater sense of responsibility for the larger "civic household." The campaign for political equality for women both altered and undermined those premises. By the 1920s, the settlement-house worker was a far less visible presence in the culture than the bobbed-hair, flapper-clad "new woman"—more independent, more athletic, more eager to compete with men, and more drawn to men's company.

Consumer Culture

These new women were both the objects and the subjects of the last major domains of society to be reorganized in this period, the industries of entertainment and consumption. Both grew dramatically between 1900 and 1929. It was one of the most important discoveries of the age that even pleasure could be engineered. Moviemakers like D. W. Griffith learned not simply to film a gripping story, but, through new techniques of scene cutting, to pace and manipulate the very emotions of their audiences.

Psychology moved into advertisements as goods and pleasures were made to sell themselves by their brands and slogans. Music halls, chain-managed vaudeville, amusement parks, dance clubs, the glittering movie palaces of the 1910s and 1920s, and, finally, radio transformed entertainment in this period, particularly for urban Americans. By the 1920s they lived in a culture much more cosmopolitan—with its African American jazz and dance music, Yiddish comedy, and screen idols who showcased their foreignness—more sexualized, more commercial, and more deliberately organized than any before it.

Together with the new forms of pleasure, a new flood of goods poured out of the early twentieth-century economy as production emphases shifted to mass-marketed goods and household consumers. Canned foods, refrigerators and other electric appliances, factory-made shirtwaists, celluloid collars, and chemically made rayon, cigarettes and soft drinks, snapshot cameras and phonograph records, together with hundreds of other consumer goods brought the reorganization of capital, production, and advertising into daily life. The most revolutionary of the era's new goods was the automobile, no longer a toy of the elites but a democratic commodity, thanks in part to Henry Ford's determination to make cars so efficiently and to pay his workers enough that even factory workers could own one. By 1929 there was one automobile for every five persons in the United States. Already the automobile's effects on the patterns of suburban living, recreation, status, rural isolation, and even sex were being acutely sensed.

By the end of the era, to be outside the new world of mass-marketed goods—as millions of poor and rural Americans continued to be—was for the first time to be an outsider in one's own nation. Almost no one in the fall of 1929 thought that the bounty might be at its end.

7

Corporate Capture Threatens Democratic Government

Liz Kennedy

Liz Kennedy is a voting rights activist and an attorney in the Democracy Program at the Brennan Center for Justice. She served as deputy director of voter protection for the 2008 Obama campaign.

In this viewpoint, voting rights expert Liz Kennedy demonstrates how the influence of corporate money on elections and other government functions can threaten the integrity of the democratic process. When big money dominates public institutions, government is prevented from being responsive to citizens. Polls have shown that a majority of Americans believe corporations have too much influence on their government.

America faces a crisis of corporate capture of democratic government, where the economic power of corporations has been translated into political power with disastrous effects for people's lives. In his new book, *Captured: The Corporate Infiltration of American Democracy*, Sen. Sheldon Whitehouse (D-RI) warns that "corporations of vast wealth and remorseless staying power have moved into our politics to seize for themselves advantages that can be seized only by control over government." The book illustrates what he calls, the "immense pressure deployed by the corporate sector in our government." We must rebalance our

"Corporate Capture Threatens Democratic Government," by Liz Kennedy, Center for American Progress, March 29, 2017. Reprinted by permission.

democracy by changing the rules to limit the power of money over government and empower people to engage politically as a countervailing force.

Currently, the domination of big money over our public institutions prevents government from being responsive to Americans. This certainly is not a new phenomenon—but it is growing. Even in 2009, before the *Citizens United v. FEC* ruling removed constraints on corporate political spending, 80 percent of Americans agreed with the following statement:

> *I am worried that large political contributions will prevent Congress from tackling the important issues facing American today, like the economic crisis, rising energy costs, reforming health care, and global warming.*

In the first presidential contest after the *Citizens United* decision, 84 percent of Americans agreed that corporate political spending drowns out the voices of average Americans, and 83 percent believed that corporations and corporate CEOs have too much political power and influence. This aligns with more recent research showing that 84 percent of people think government is benefitting special interests, and 83 percent think government is benefitting big corporations and the wealthy.

As already noted, the undue influence of corporate interests on the functions of government is not new, and Sen. Whitehouse's book explains how Americans have faced and overcome this threat before. America's founders recognized the danger of corporate capture: In 1816, Thomas Jefferson warned the new republic to "crush in its birth the aristocracy of our monied corporations which dare already to challenge our government to a trial of strength, and bid defiance to the laws of their country." Almost a century later, President Theodore Roosevelt, in his annual address to Congress in 1907, said:

> *The fortunes amassed through corporate organization are now so large, and vest such power in those that wield them, as to make it a matter of necessity to give to the sovereign—that is, to*

the Government, which represents the people as a whole—some effective power of supervision over their corporate use.

President Roosevelt was responsible for the first federal ban on corporate political contributions. But now America's rules for using money in politics are out of date, and our system of government is out of balance. The Supreme Court's conservative majority has turned its back on reasonable limits for how concentrated wealth can be used to shape government and public choices. In 2010, *Citizens United* allowed corporate money to be used to support or attack candidates and influence American elections. Previously, in a case overruled by *Citizens United*, the Court upheld corporate political spending rules, decrying "the corrosive and distorting effects of immense aggregations of wealth that are accumulated with the help of the corporate form and that have little or no correlation to the public's support for the corporation's political ideas." In his book, Sen. Whitehouse calls out the Supreme Court's conservative majority, which has "obediently repaid the corporate powers by changing the basic operating systems of our democracy in ways that consistently give big corporate powers even more power in our process of government, rewiring our democracy to corporate advantage."

Corporate interests can vastly outspend labor or public interest groups on elections. For example, in 2014, business interests spent $1.1 billion on state candidates and committees compared to the $215 million that labor groups spent. That same year, business political action committees, or PACs, spent nearly $380 million in federal elections, while labor union PACs gave close to $60 million. In 2016, it is estimated that $1 out of every $8 that went to super PACs came from corporate sources. Super PACs—which didn't exist before 2010—raised almost $1.8 billion for the 2016 elections. Recently developed dark money channels have exploded, and more than $800 million dollars of political spending with no disclosure of donors has occurred since 2010. This denies voters information and blocks accountability by hiding the identity of political spenders who want to push their agendas and points of view without leaving fingerprints. Dark money has led to an increase in negative campaigning and deceptive statements in political advertisements, feeding the politics of destruction.

Moreover, the anti-democratic influence of money in politics doesn't end on election day. The dominance of corporations and business interests exists not just in election spending but also in lobbying elected officials and decision-makers. In 2012, an important study of political influence, *Unheavenly Chorus*, looked at organized-interest activity aimed at influencing policymaking in Washington, D.C. According to the study, social welfare and labor organization made up just 2 percent of all organized-interest activity—corporations, trade associations, and business groups accounted for 48 percent. Corporations and business groups spend much more on lobbying than organizations that represent large constituencies of Americans. For example, between 1998 and 2016, OpenSecrets.org reports that the US Chamber of Commerce—just one of many groups advocating for the interests of big business—spent $1.3 billion on lobbying the federal government compared to $720 million spent by all labor unions.

Corporate influence over government does not end with the passing of a law. Corporate entities with no natural limits and endless resources can wage a long-term, sustained attack across policymaking pressure points. For example, if a law is passed that corporate interests oppose, relentless industry pressure can be brought to bear on the agencies charged with enforcing that legislation. Again, in his book, Sen. Whitehouse describes "heavy lawyering of the rulemaking and enforcement processes, often as simple brute pressure to cause delay and cost" on the part of corporate interests. Furthermore, any final rule may be challenged in courts that are increasingly friendly to corporate forces at the expense of people.

In the short time that President Donald Trump has been in office, the revolving door between industry and the federal agencies regulating them is back in full swing thanks to the administration loosening restrictions on lobbyists taking posts at agencies they previously sought to influence on behalf corporate clients. The independent nonprofit newsroom ProPublica discovered dozens of federally registered lobbyists who were among the first Trump appointees to take positions in federal agencies. For example, lobbyists for the pharmaceutical industry and health insurance companies are now in key posts at the US Department of Health and Human Services; a lobbyist for the construction industry who fought wage and worker safety standards now works for the US Department of Labor; a lobbyist for the extractive resources industry is now at the US Department of Energy; and a for-profit college lobbyist who sought to weaken protections for students worked at the US Department of Education.

In the Trump administration, as noted by Eric Lipton at the *New York Times*, we continue to see "the merging of private business interest with government affairs." In just one example, billionaire investor Carl Icahn has been named "special adviser to the president," but because he is not officially a government employee, he is not subject to the same conflict of interest divestment requirements. As a consequence, Icahn maintains his majority holdings in an oil refinery while zealously advocating for a rule change that would have saved his refinery more than $200 million the previous year. We have reached an apotheosis of concentrated wealth running government for their interests—Trump's cabinet has more wealth than one-third of American households, and Icahn is wealthier than all of them combined.

Captured: The Corporate Infiltration of American Democracy tells hard truths about the central threat posed by the rule of the rich—plutocracy—and how it is overwhelming American democracy. Sen. Whitehouse writes, "Corporate money is calling the tune in Congress; Congress is unwilling or unable to stand up to corporate power (indeed, Congress is often its agent)." These are truths that must be faced to be fixed.

Corporate Capture Threatens Democratic Government

Our democratic society must demonstrate its resilience and return to core American principles and values of government that serve the people. We have the power to demand that Congress break the nexus between Wall Street and Washington that keeps the rules of our economy rigged to benefit the wealthiest few at the expense of the many. Americans can resist the slide to secret political spending and require disclosure for the big money interests behind our toxic politics of personal destruction. We can demand that lobbyists be prohibited from acting as fundraisers. And, amidst the shocking scandal of Russian interference in America's democracy, we can insist that Congress ban foreign corporate money in elections.

Let us harbor no illusions—this battle won't be easy, but that doesn't mean it is impossible. Ever since our founding as a republic, Americans have fought to expand democratic freedoms and protect democratic society from being corrupted through unchecked private greed and undermined through grotesque inequality. One can clearly see the result of corporate power over policy in the present levels of wealth inequality—unmatched since the Great Depression—where all the economic gains in the past several years accrued to the wealthiest 1 percent. But as economist Thomas Piketty concluded his study of economic inequality in *Capital in the Twenty-First Century* by writing, "If we are to regain control of capitalism, we must bet everything on democracy."

For democracy to work, the rules must be rewritten to prevent corporate capture of government and to create a system that supports fair representation for all Americans. Whether we fight to preserve our free system of self-government for ourselves and posterity is not a choice—it is a moral obligation.

8

Privatization and Corporate Wealth in the Late Twentieth Century

Sarah Anderson and John Cavanagh

Sarah Anderson and John Cavanagh are co-directors of the Global Economy Project at the Institute of Policy Studies.

Although the data in this classic article is somewhat dated, the authors offer a detailed and fact-driven overview of wealth trends that left a major impression on American life in the early twenty-first century. Many of those who describe the contemporary American economy in oligarchic terms point to such trends as evidence.

As citizen movements the world over launch activities to counter aspects of economic globalization, the growing power of private corporations is becoming a central issue.

Key Findings

1. Of the 100 largest economies in the world, 51 are corporations; only 49 are countries (based on a comparison of corporate sales and country GDPs).
2. The Top 200 corporations' sales are growing at a faster rate than overall global economic activity. Between 1983 and 1999, their combined sales grew from the equivalent of 25.0 percent to 27.5 percent of World GDP.

"Top 200: The Rise of Corporate Global Power," by Sarah Anderson and John Cavanagh, Institute for Policy Studies, December 4, 2000. Reprinted by permission.

3. The Top 200 corporations' combined sales are bigger than the combined economies of all countries minus the biggest 10.
4. The Top 200s' combined sales are 18 times the size of the combined annual income of the 1.2 billion people (24 percent of the total world population) living in "severe" poverty.
5. While the sales of the Top 200 are the equivalent of 27.5 percent of world economic activity, they employ only 0.78 percent of the world's workforce.
6. Between 1983 and 1999, the profits of the Top 200 firms grew 362.4 percent, while the number of people they employ grew by only 14.4 percent.
7. A full 5 percent of the Top 200s' combined workforce is employed by Wal-Mart, a company notorious for union-busting and widespread use of part-time workers to avoid paying benefits. The discount retail giant is the top private employer in the world, with 1,140,000 workers—more than twice as many as No. 2, DaimlerChrysler, which employs 466,938.
8. US corporations dominate the Top 200, with 82 slots (41 percent of the total). Japanese firms are second, with only 41 slots.
9. Of the US corporations on the list, 44 did not pay the full standard 35 percent federal corporate tax rate during the period 1996–1998. Seven of the firms actually paid less than zero in federal income taxes in 1998 (because of rebates). These include: Texaco, Chevron, PepsiCo, Enron, Worldcom, McKesson and the world's biggest corporation—General Motors.
10. Between 1983 and 1999, the share of total sales of the Top 200 made up by service sector corporations increased from 33.8 percent to 46.7 percent. Gains were particularly evident in financial services and

telecommunications sectors, in which most countries have pursued deregulation.

Introduction

In 1952, General Motors CEO Charles Wilson made the famous statement that "What is good for General Motors is good for the country." During the past decade and a half, General Motors and other global corporations have obtained much of what they claimed was good for them. They have succeeded in obtaining trade and investment liberalization policies that provide global firms considerable new freedoms to pursue profits internationally. They have also persuaded governments to take a generally hands-off approach to corporate monopolies, claiming that mega-mergers are needed for firms to compete in global markets.

This study examines the economic and political power of the world's top 200 corporations. Led by General Motors, these are the firms that are driving the process of corporate globalization and arguably benefiting the most from it. The report then examines the extent to which these firms are fulfilling the second half of Charles Wilson's promise by providing "what's good for the country" and global society in general. The conclusion of our analysis is that widespread trade and investment liberalization have contributed to a climate in which dominant corporations are enjoying increasing levels of economic and political clout that are out of balance with the tangible benefits they provide to society.

The study reinforces a strong public distrust of the economic and political power of corporations. In September 2000, *Business Week* magazine released a Business Week/Harris Poll which showed that between 72 and 82 percent of Americans agree that "Business has gained too much power over too many aspects of American life." In the same poll, 74 percent of Americans agreed with Vice President Al Gore's criticism of "a wide range of large corporations, including big tobacco, big oil, the big polluters, the pharmaceutical companies, the HMOs." And, 74-82 percent agreed that big companies have too much influence over "government policy, politicians, and policy-makers in Washington."

Overview of the Top 200

US Firms Lead the Pack

Top US firms faced stiff competition from Japanese corporations throughout much of the late 1980s and early 1990s. In 1995, Japanese and US firms were nearly tied in the number of corporations on the Top 200 list, with 58 and 59, respectively. Because the Japanese economy has been in stagnation for nearly a decade, US corporations are once again dominant, comprising 41 percent of the Top 200 in 1999. The countries with the most corporations on the Top 200 list are the United States (82), Japan (41), Germany (20), and France (17).

Fewer Firms Outside the Industrial Giants

In 1999, South Korea was the only country with a corporation on the Top 200 list outside North America, Japan, and Europe. In 1983, Brazil, Israel, South Africa, and India also had firms on the list. The merger boom of the past two decades, particularly among US firms but also in Europe, has further concentrated economic power in companies based in the leading industrial economies. For example, two of the top five firms in 1999 were the products of mega-mergers: Exxon Mobil (No. 2) and DaimlerChrysler (No. 5).

Services on the Rise

The types of firms in the Top 200 also reflect trends in the global economy. During the past decade and a half, the World Bank and International Monetary Fund have promoted reforms to lift controls on investment in banking, telecommunications, and other services, opening new markets for the global giants in these sectors. Hence, the former dominance of manufacturing and natural resource-based corporations among the Top 200 has eroded. Between 1983 and 1999, the share of total sales of the Top 200 made up by service corporations increased from 33.8 percent to 46.7 percent. One major firm, General Electric, helped bolster the service sector component of the list. While GE is best known for appliances, its financial services division has grown so large (at least half of sales) that the company has shifted from the manufacturing to the services category.

Concentration

In 1999, more than half the sales of the Top 200 were in just 4 economic sectors: financial services (14.5 percent), motor vehicles and parts (12.7 percent), insurance (12.4 percent), and retailing/wholesaling (11.3 percent).

Stability at the Top

Despite some noteworthy shifts, more than half of the firms that were on the Top 200 list in 1983 made the cut again in 1999. Returnees totaled 103, although in 25 cases they were listed under a different name, due to mergers, spin-offs, and name changes. The most stunning ascendance among the Top 200 firms is that of Wal-Mart. In 1983, the retail giant's sales were $4.7 billion—far below the Top 200 threshold. By 1999, they had climbed to $166.8 billion, making Wal-Mart the second largest firm in the world.

Power of the Top 200
Economic Clout

Top 200 vs. Countries

- Of the 100 largest economies in the world, 51 are corporations; only 49 are countries (based on a comparison of corporate sales and country GDPs). To put this in perspective, General Motors is now bigger than Denmark; DaimlerChrysler is bigger than Poland; Royal Dutch/Shell is bigger than Venezuela; IBM is bigger than Singapore; and Sony is bigger than Pakistan.
- The 1999 sales of each of the top five corporations (General Motors, Wal-Mart, Exxon Mobil, Ford Motor, and DaimlerChrysler) are bigger than the GDP's of 182 countries.

- The Top 200 corporations' combined sales are bigger than the combined economies of all countries minus the biggest 10.

Top 200 Growing Faster Than Rest of World

The Top 200 corporations' sales are growing at a faster rate than overall global economic activity. Between 1983 and 1999, their combined sales grew from the equivalent of 25.0% to 27.5% of World GDP.

Top 200 vs. the World's Poorest

The economic clout of the Top 200 is particularly staggering compared to that of the poorest segment of the world's humanity. The Top 200s' combined sales are 18 times the size of the combined annual income of the 1.2 billion people (24 percent of the total world population) living in "severe" poverty (defined by the World Bank as those surviving on less than $1 per day).

Political Clout

Campaign Contributions

The 82 US companies on the Top 200 list made contributions to 2000 election campaigns through political action committees (not including soft money donations) that totaled $33,045,832. According to the Center for Responsive Politics, corporations in general outspent labor unions by a ratio of about 15-to-1. The group also found that candidates for the US House of Representatives who outspent their opponents were victorious in 94 percent of their races. Unfortunately, campaign contribution data for non-US firms is not available.

Lobbying

Of course global corporations also spend massive amounts each year influencing the political system through lobbying. The exact amount spent on these activities is not known, but of the Top 200 firms, 94 maintain "government relations" offices located on or within a few blocks of the lobbying capital of the world—Washington, DC's K Street Corridor.

USTR Inc.
Campaign contributions and lobbying are only the most visible example of corporate political clout. For example, officials with the US Trade Representative's (USTR) Office, who are responsible for negotiating international trade and investment agreements, routinely state that their primary responsibility is to represent the interests of US industry, rather than all Americans affected by trade deals. This in spite of the fact that the USTR, upon its creation in 1960, was deliberately placed in the White House, rather than the Commerce Department, in order to prevent it from being overly influenced by business interests. In addition, trade negotiators are required to meet with nongovernmental advisory committees, but these are overwhelmingly dominated by representatives of large corporations. Recently, the US government went a step further and allowed representatives from corporations such as AT&T and IBM to join the official delegation in hemispheric talks on electronic commerce in the Free Trade Area of the Americas, which is due to be finalized by 2005.

Transparency
The political influence of top firms is also evident in the scarcity of publicly available information on their activities. Leading corporations have fiercely opposed attempts to require them to achieve a higher level of transparency. Just a few examples of information that US firms are not required to reveal to the American public:

- a breakdown of their employees by country
- toxic emissions at overseas plants
- locations of overseas plants or contractors
- wage rates at overseas facilities
- layoffs and the reasons for layoffs

In most cases, collecting company-specific data in countries outside the United States is even more difficult.

Contributions of the Top 200

This section looks at the contributions the Top 200 corporations make to society in terms of jobs and taxes. This is not to deny that these firms may influence our lives in many other ways. Particularly in the United States and other rich nations, it is difficult to go through a day without direct contact with many of these companies, whether you are watching a movie, shopping in a supermarket, driving a car, or depositing a check.

Nevertheless, given their extreme levels of economic and political power, it is important to take a hard look at whether these corporate giants are indeed upholding their end of the social compact. The corporations themselves, when lobbying for policies to lift barriers to trade and investment, have promised that they will lead not only to improved consumer goods and services but also to significant job creation and an overall improvement in social welfare. It seems only fair that the public should be able to expect—at a minimum—that these colossal firms be major providers of employment opportunities and that they bear their share of the tax burden.

Jobs

Sales vs. Workers

While the sales of the Top 200 are the equivalent of 27.5% of world economic activity, these firms employ only a tiny fraction of the world's workers. In 1999, they employed a combined total of 22,682,166 workers, which is 0.78% of the world's workforce.

Profit vs. Employment Growth

Between 1983 and 1999, the number of people employed by Top 200 firms grew 14.4%, an increase that is dwarfed by the firms' 362.4% profit growth over this period.

Corporate analysts may see the dramatic increase in the ratio between profits and employees as a positive sign of increased efficiency. The growing gap between profits and payrolls is at least partly the result of technological changes that has allowed firms to produce more with less people. Automation is not always a negative development, especially in the case of jobs that are dangerous or otherwise undesirable. However, another factor is the trend towards outsourcing, particularly among large industrial firms. By shifting more and more of their production to contractors, companies can distance themselves from potential charges of labor rights abuses and other illegal behavior and keep labor costs low by forcing contractors to compete for business with an ever smaller number of giant purchasers. The giant firms also have more freedom to hire and fire contractors to meet shifting demand. US corporations have been at the forefront of this trend.

Chrysler (known as DaimlerChrsyler since the merger with Daimler Benz), for example, purchases almost all of its parts, from brakes to seats, from suppliers. Hewlett-Packard relies on 10 different contractors and IBM relies on 8 to make their products. In recent years, Japanese electronics firms, including Mitsubishi, NEC, Fujitsu, and Sony, have also begun to outsource.

Still, Americans may be less concerned about the growing gap between profits and employees because of the country's record low unemployment rate. What is often ignored in the mainstream media is the fact that unemployment problems remain prevalent elsewhere in the world, including in many countries where the Top 200 firms are enjoying strong profits. (US firms overall earned 19 percent of their profits overseas in 1995.) In the European Union, the 1999 unemployment rate was 10 percent, compared to 4.2 percent in the United States. The International Labor Organization estimates that one billion people worldwide are unemployed or underemployed. Joblessness around the world hurts the United States because it reduces the capacity of consumers in other countries to purchase US products and can lead to social instability that has international ramifications.

Wal-Mart Workers

A full 5 percent of the Top 200s' combined workforce is comprised of Wal-Mart employees. The discount retail giant's workforce has skyrocketed from 62,000 in 1983 to 1,140,000 in 1999, making it the largest private employer in the world. The next largest, DaimlerChrysler, has a workforce of 466,938—less than half the size of Wal-Mart's. Although Wal-Mart is indeed providing many new jobs, the company is notorious for its strategy of employing armies of workers on a part-time basis to avoid paying benefits. The firm is also adamantly anti-union. In March, Wal-Mart announced it was closing the meat department in 180 stores two weeks after the meat cutters at one Texas store voted to form a union—the first successful organizing drive at an American Wal-Mart.

Taxes

Not Too Big to Hide from Tax Collectors

The Institute on Taxation and Economic Policy (ITEP) recently released a study of federal tax rates paid by several hundred major, profitable US corporations. Forty-four of the US corporations on the Top 200 list were included in the study, which revealed that not a single one of them had paid the full standard 35 percent corporate tax rate during the period 1996-1998. Seven of the firms had actually paid less than zero in federal income taxes in 1998, because they received rebates that exceeded the amount of taxes they paid. These include: Texaco, Chevron, PepsiCo, Enron, Worldcom, McKesson and the world's biggest corporation—General Motors. According to ITEP, companies use a variety of means to lower their federal income taxes, including tax credits for activities like research and oil drilling and accelerated depreciation write-offs.

Tax Avoidance Internationally

While company-specific data on tax avoidance outside the United States does not exist, the trend towards lower corporate tax burdens is also evident internationally. According to the OECD, over the past two decades the share of total taxes made up by corporate income tax in the industrialized OECD countries has remained about 8 percent, despite strong increases in corporate profits. The organization attributes this decline in tax rates to the use of "tax havens" and intense competition among industrialized countries as they attempt to lure investment by offering lower taxes.

Conclusion

As citizen movements the world over launch activities to counter aspects of economic globalization, the growing power of private corporations is becoming a central issue. The main beneficiaries of the market-opening policies of the major multilateral institutions over the past decade and a half are these large corporations, especially the top 200.

This growing private power has enormous economic consequences, spelled out in this report. However, the greatest impact may be political, as corporations transform economic clout into political power. As a result, democracy is undermined. This threat deserves to be one of the major issues on the political agenda in the United States and overseas.

9

We Should Be Investing in People and Things Other Than War

Jake Johnson

Jake Johnson is a staff writer at Common Dreams and an agenda contributor at the World Economic Forum. His work focuses on inequality, corporate malfeasance, and progressive politics.

In this viewpoint, Jake Johnson examines how Senator Bernie Sanders has leveraged wealth inequality and perceived oligarchic economic conditions as the centerpiece of his platform and political identity. Sanders argues that inequality and corruption go hand-in-hand with authoritarianism and oligarchy. The US political and economic system is controlled by an elite group of billionaires. Instead, the people should have that power, and this can only be achieved by investing in children, education, the elderly, and health care, rather than in war.

In a wide-ranging speech viewed by more than 11,000 people from over 30 countries, Sen. Bernie Sanders (I-Vt.) on Sunday commemorated the 15th anniversary of the US invasion of Iraq by highlighting its devastating consequences and issuing an urgent call for a global agenda that pursues "peace, not war" and "development, not destruction."

"In #CallForPeace Address, Sanders Takes On Endless War and Global Oligarchy," by Jake Johnson, Common Dreams, March 18, 2018. https://www.commondreams.org/news/2018/03/18/callforpeace-address-sanders-denounces-endless-war-and-rise-oligarchy. Licensed under CC BY-SA 3.0.

"We need to invest in our children, in our elderly, and in healthcare and education and environmental protection. We do not want more and more war," Sanders said. "People in my country, the United States, and all over the world are sick and tired of spending billions and billions of dollars on nuclear weapons, war planes, missiles, bombs, and tanks."

Sanders—who was joined on Sunday at the #CallForPeace event by Korea expert and peace activist Christine Ahn, Raed Jarrar of Amnesty International, and Jenny Town of the US-Korea Institute—also used his speech to highlight global crises ranging from human-caused climate change to the rise of oligarchy.

"Increasingly, in the United States and around the world, we see an economic and political system in which a small number of multi-billionaires and corporate interests have increased control over the world's economic life, our political life, and our media," Sanders said. "Inequality, corruption, oligarchy, and authoritarianism are inseparable. They must be understood as part of the same system, and fought and opposed in the same way."

These are crises that can only be solved through international cooperation, not unilateral action by powerful nations, Sanders argues.

"The threat of climate change is a very clear example of why we all need to pull together, we are in this together. The United States can't do it alone, Europe can't do it alone, China can't do it alone, no one country can do this alone," Sanders concluded. "This is a crisis that calls out for strong international cooperation if we are to leave our children and our grandchildren a planet that is healthy and habitable."

A full transcript of [Sanders's] speech follows.

Let me thank you very much, and let me thank MoveOn for helping to organize this event and thank all of the people throughout the world for coming together. I think we all understand that the great global crises are not going to be solved country by country. They're only going to be solved when millions and hundreds of

We Should Be Investing in People and Things Other Than War

millions of people come together to demand a fundamental change in global priorities, and certainly at the top of that list is the need to end war and destruction, and work toward a global peace.

So again, I want to thank everybody for the work they are doing, we're all in this together.

Today, we are here to mark a very somber anniversary, and that is the beginning of the Iraq War in 2003. Fifteen years ago this week, the bombs started falling on Baghdad; "shock and awe" was what the Bush administration called it, and the news media repeated it, creating the expectation that US military power would make the war quick and easy. We all remember that.

The theory was that Saddam Hussein would be overthrown in a few weeks, democracy in Iraq would be established, American troops would return home in a few months, and everything would be wonderful from then on out.

Well, it didn't quite happen like that.

Later we would all be shocked and awed at the disaster they had created, because war is never quick, and it is never easy.

I remember vividly—I was in Congress at the time—all of the rhetoric that came from the Bush administration, that came from my Republican colleagues and some Democrats as well, about why going to war in Iraq was the right thing to do.

Well, it wasn't.

In fact, it is one of the great tragedies in modern history. It is very easy to give speeches in the safety of the floor of the Senate or in the House; it is a little bit harder to experience war and live through the devastation of war, and to deal with the aftermath, the consequences.

I was one of those that opposed the war at the beginning. Today, it is now broadly acknowledged that the war in Iraq was a foreign policy blunder of enormous magnitude.

The war created a cascade of instability around the region that we are still dealing with today in Syria and elsewhere, and will be for many years to come.

Indeed, had it not been for the Iraq War, ISIS would almost certainly not exist.

The war deepened hostilities between Sunni and Shia communities in Iraq and elsewhere; it exacerbated a regional struggle for power between Saudi Arabia and Iran and their proxies in places like Syria, Lebanon, and Yemen; and it undermined American diplomatic efforts to resolve the Israeli-Palestinian conflict.

The devastation experienced by Iraq's civilians was unbelievable. A recent academic study by US, Canadian, and Iraqi researchers found that over 400,000 Iraqi civilians—nearly half a million people—were killed directly or indirectly as a consequence of the war [note: other researchers have estimated that the total number of deaths from the war exceeds one million].

The war led to the deaths of some 4,400 US troops and the wounding, physical and emotional, of tens of thousands of others.

The war led to the displacement of nearly five million people both inside and outside of Iraq, putting great stress on the ability of surrounding countries to deal with these refugee flows.

We've also seen this more recently in Europe, as the large numbers of people fleeing the Syrian war has generated a backlash in European countries, giving rise to anti-Muslim and anti-immigrant sentiments that have been exploited by right-wing politicians.

And, by the way, that war in Iraq cost trillions of dollars—money that could have been spent on addressing the massive levels of poverty and hopelessness that exists all over the developing world, where hundreds of millions of people today live in extreme poverty and where many children around the world die as a result of easily prevented diseases.

The Iraq War, like so many other military conflicts, had unintended consequences. It ended up making us less safe, not more safe.

The Iraq War also set a precedent—a very dangerous precedent—that large countries like the United States could attack small countries with impunity. Instead of moving us forward to a world without war, where international conflicts are settled through negotiations and diplomacy, we now see wars all over the world and a significant increase in global military spending.

For example, right here in the United States, Congress just voted to increase the Defense Department budget by $165 billion over a two-year period.

No one disagrees that Saddam Hussein was a brutal, murderous dictator. But it's now known that he had nothing to do with 9/11. The American people were misled by the Bush administration into believing that the Iraq War was necessary to prevent another 9/11.

Forty years before that, in 1964, President Lyndon Johnson cited an attack on a US ship in the Gulf of Tonkin as a pretext for escalating US intervention in Vietnam. We now know that his administration misled both Congress and the American people into that war, just as the Bush administration did in Iraq.

Time and time again, we see disasters when leaders refuse to tell their people the truth. And let's remember that the people of the world were not silent about the Iraq War.

In the months leading up to the invasion, there were huge and unprecedented demonstrations in the United States, and in fact all over the world, opposing that war.

The truth is that in country after country, what people were saying is that we need to invest in our children, in our elderly, and in healthcare and education and environmental protection. We do not want more and more war.

People in my country, the United States, and all over the world are sick and tired of spending billions and billions of dollars on nuclear weapons, war planes, missiles, bombs, and tanks.

Our job together, in each of our countries, is to bring our people together around an agenda that calls for peace, not war; development, not destruction.

Let me say a brief word about some of the shared global challenges that we face today.

The growth of oligarchy and income and wealth inequality is not just an American issue; it is a global issue.

Globally, the top one percent now owns more wealth than the bottom 99 percent of the world's population.

Increasingly, in the United States and around the world, we see an economic and political system in which a small number of multi-billionaires and corporate interests have increased control over the world's economic life, our political life, and our media.

And these people are working night and day just to make themselves even richer.

Just a few years ago, it was estimated that the wealthiest people and the most profitable corporations in the world have stashed at least $21 trillion in offshore tax havens to avoid paying their fair share of taxes.

The situation has become so absurd that one five-story building in the Cayman Islands, which has a zero percent corporate tax rate, is now the home of nearly 20,000 companies.

In other words, while the very, very rich become much richer, governments around the world institute austerity programs, because they lack the funds to provide decently for their constituents.

Inequality, corruption, oligarchy, and authoritarianism are inseparable. They must be understood as part of the same system, and fought and opposed in the same way.

Around the world, we have witnessed the rise of demagogues, who once in power use their positions to loot the state of its resources. These kleptocrats like Putin in Russia and many others use divisiveness and abuse as a tool for enriching themselves and those loyal to them.

The last years have obviously seen very troubling political developments in many countries around the world, particularly in Europe and also here in the United States.

The rise of intolerant, authoritarian political movements is something that should concern each and every one of us.

These movements have drawn strength from the fact that more and more people have lost faith in their systems of government and are desperate for alternatives.

They see their governments as corrupt, ineffective, and not delivering for them or providing opportunities for a better future for their children.

The problem is, when you see leaders that tell the people, "I, only I, can deliver you security, opportunity, and a future. It's those people over there that are taking it away from you."

They point to politically unpopular groups, ethnic and religious minorities, immigrants, refugees, and blame these groups for all the trouble, and then propose to strip these groups of their rights.

That is how demagogues work. They gain power by claiming to speak to people's legitimate desires, but always end up using that power to oppress them. They claim to speak for the many, but really represent the very few.

We have seen this played out before many times in history.

Further, we cannot forget, when we talk about global crises, the crisis of climate change.

My friends, it is time for us to get serious about this issue. The scientific community is virtually unanimous in telling us that climate change is real, it is caused by human activity, and it is already causing devastating harm throughout the world.

Further, what the scientists tell us is that if we do not act boldly, together, to address this crisis of climate change, this planet will see more drought, more floods, and more types of devastation.

Furthermore, what we will see is a level of migration, of people moving away from areas where they cannot grow foods or drinkable water, which will cause all kinds of other threats to global stability and security.

The threat of climate change is a very clear example of why we all need to pull together, we are in this together. The United States can't do it alone, Europe can't do it alone, China can't do it alone, and no one country can do this alone.

This is a crisis that calls out for strong international cooperation if we are to leave our children and our grandchildren a planet that is healthy and habitable.

So let me just conclude by again thanking all of you who are watching this program, who understand that we need to stand together, to rally the people for social, economic, political, and racial justice, and that the only way we are going to solve international problems is when people throughout the world come together.

10

The US Has a Government of, by, and for Billionaires

Bernie Sanders

Vermont's Senator Bernie Sanders is a former candidate for president and an icon of the progressive movement in America.

In the following excerpted transcript of a conversation with journalist E. J. Dionne Jr. (an event that took place several years before the speech referenced in the previous viewpoint), Senator Bernie Sanders paints a grim picture of contemporary American life. Sanders had just released a 12-point Agenda for America addressing the nation's pressing economic challenges. His agenda spanned infrastructure investment, climate change, wage growth, affordable college and health care, tax reform, and expansion of Social Security, Medicare, and Medicaid.

On Saturday, just this last Saturday, I had been invited to speak in Harrisburg, Pennsylvania, and my friend and I, we're driving back to D.C., and we drove through Gettysburg, and we stopped there for a while at the Battlefield of Monuments and the Museum, and while we were there we of course saw the Lincoln statues and we read from his Gettysburg Address. And you all know about Lincoln's extraordinary Gettysburg Address where he said a hell of a lot more than I said in ten times as much time

Transcript from "An Economic Agenda for America: A Conversation with Senator Bernie Sanders," by Bernie Sanders and E. J. Dionne, Jr. The Brookings Institution, February 9, 2015. Reprinted by permission.

Is America a Democracy or an Oligarchy?

as he said it, but he said of a hope that this nation would have "a new birth of freedom and that government of the people, by the people, and for the people shall not perish from the earth." What an extraordinary statement.

And as we drove back from Gettysburg to Washington it struck me hard that Lincoln's extraordinary vision, a government of the people, by the people, for the people was, in fact, perishing, was coming to an end, and that we are moving rapidly away from our democratic heritage into an oligarchic form of society where today we are experiencing a government of the billionaires, by the billionaires, and for the billionaires.

Today, in my view, the most serious problem we face as a nation is the grotesque and growing level of wealth and income inequality. This is a profound moral issue. It is an economic issue, and it is a political issue. Economically for the last 40 years the great middle class of our country, once the envy of the world, has been in decline despite—and here's the important point to make that we have got to answer—despite an explosion of technology, despite a huge increase in productivity, despite all the so-called benefits of the global economy, millions of American workers today are working longer hours for low wages, and we have more people living in poverty than almost any time in the history of our country.

Today real unemployment is not the 5.7 percent you read in the newspapers. It is 11.3 percent if you include those people who are working part-time when they want to work full-time or those people who have given up looking for work entirely. We don't talk about it. Pope Francis does by the way, but we don't talk about the fact that youth unemployment in this country is 18 percent, and African-American youth unemployment is nearly 30 percent.

Shamefully we have by far the highest rate of childhood poverty of any major country on earth. You hear a whole lot of discussion about family values from our Republican friends but nothing about the fact that almost 20 percent of our kids are living in poverty.

Despite the modest success of the Affordable Care Act some 40 million Americans continue to have no health insurance while even more are underinsured with high deductibles, high co-payments, high premiums. We remain today the only major country on earth that does not guarantee health care to all people as a right, and yet we end up spending almost twice as much per person on health care as do the people of any other nation.

Now, as all of you know there are a lot of angry people out there all across the country. Some of them are in the Occupy Wall Street Movement and consider themselves Progressives. Some are in the Tea Party Movement and consider themselves Conservatives, but let me give you an explanation as to why they have every right in the world to be angry.

Since 1999 the typical middle-class family, that family right in the middle of the economy, has seen its income go down by almost $5,000 after adjusting for inflation. Incredibly that family earned less income last year than it did 26 years ago back in 1989. The median male worker, that guy right in the middle of the economy, made $783 less last year than he did 42 years ago, while the median female worker earned $1,300 less last year than she did in 2007.

That is why people are angry. They're working longer hours for lower wages. They're seeing an explosion of technology. They're watching TV and seeing all the great benefits supposedly of the global economy, and they're working long hours for low wages, and they're scared to death as to what is going to happen to their kids. What kinds of jobs are their kids going to have?

Are we better off today economically than we were six years ago when President Bush left office? Of course we are, but anyone who doesn't understand the suffering, anxiety, and fear that the middle-class and working families of our country are experiencing today has no idea about what's going on in the economy, and I fear very much a lot of the pundits here on Capitol Hill don't understand that. It might be a good idea to get off of Capitol—go into the real world and find out what's going on with working people.

Meanwhile, while the middle class continues to disappear, the wealthiest people in this country and the largest corporations are doing phenomenally well, and the gap between the very, very rich and everybody else is growing wider and wider. The top 1 percent now own about 41 percent of the entire wealth of the United States, while the bottom 60 percent own less than 2 percent of our wealth.

And this one is incredible: today the top 1/10th of 1 percent—that is the wealthiest 16,000 families—now own almost as much wealth as the bottom 90 percent. One-tenth of 1 percent owns almost as much wealth as the bottom 90 percent. Is that really what the United States of America is supposed to be about? I don't think so and I don't think most Americans think so. Today the Walton family, the owners of Walmart, and the wealthiest family in America are now worth about $153 billion. That one family owns more wealth than the bottom 40 percent of the American people.

In terms of income as opposed to wealth, almost all of the new income generated in recent years has gone to the top 1 percent. In fact, the latest information that we have shows that in recent years over 99 percent of all new income generated in the economy has gone to the top 1 percent. In other words, for the middle class, GDP doesn't matter. Two percent, 4 percent, 6 percent; doesn't matter. Just the middle-class and working families are not getting any of it. It's all going to the top 1 percent.

In other words while millions of Americans saw a decline in their family income, while we have seen an increase in senior poverty throughout this country, over 99 percent of all the new income generated goes to the top 1 percent. An example: the top 25 hedge-fund managers made more than $24 billion in 2013. That is equivalent to the full salaries of more than 425,000 public school teachers. Anyone really think that is morally acceptable? Economically acceptable? Is that really what our country should be about?

But income inequality is not just the moral issue of whether we are satisfied about living in a country where we have seen a proliferation of billionaires at the same time as millions of families are struggling to make sure they're able to feed their kids. It is also a profound political issue.

As a result of the disastrous Supreme Court decision, the five to four decision on *Citizens United*, billionaire families are now able to spend hundreds and hundreds of millions of dollars to purchase the candidates of their choice. The billionaire class now owns the economy, and they are working day and night to make certain that they own the United States government.

According to media reports it appears that one family, the extreme right wing Koch Brothers, are prepared to spend more money than either the Democratic Party or the Republican Party in the coming elections. In other words, one family, a family which is worth about $100 billion, may well have a stronger political presence than either of our major parties.

Now, I know that people are not comfortable when I say this, but I want you to take a hard look at what's going on, take a deep breath, and you tell me whether or not we are looking at a democracy or whether or not we are looking at an oligarchy when you have one family that has more political power than the Democratic Party, than the Republican Party, which can spend unlimited sums of money not only on campaigns but on think tanks, on media. I worry very, very much about the future of democracy in our country, and that is why it is absolutely imperative that we pass a Constitutional Amendment to overturn *Citizens United*, and in fact why we must move forward to a public funding of elections. I want young people out there, whatever their point of view may be who like the idea of public service to be able to run for office, to get involved in politics without having to worry about sucking up to billionaires in order to get the support that they may need.

Now, given the economic crisis that we face—I talked a little bit about the political crisis. Given the economic crisis that I laid out a little bit of what that's about. Where do we go? What should we be doing? How do we rebuild the disappearing middle class and create an economy that works for all of our people?

Is America a Democracy or an Oligarchy?

[...]

In today's highly competitive global economy millions of Americans are unable to afford the higher education they need in order to get good paying jobs. All of you know that hundreds of thousands of young people have literally given up on the dream of going to college while others are graduating school deeply, deeply in debt. A few months ago I met with a woman in Burlington, Vermont. Her crime was that she went to medical school to become a primary-care physician for low-income people. That was her crime, and the result of that crime was that she has $300,000 in debt. That is nuts, and what we have got to learn is that in countries like Germany, Scandinavia, many part of the world, people are competing against us, they are smart enough to understand that the future of their countries depends on the education their young people get. Their college education and graduate school is free. We've got to learn that lesson. Free public education does not have to end at high school. President Obama's initiative for two years of community college is good start. We have got to go further as a nation.

We cannot run away from the fact that the greed and recklessness and illegal behavior on Wall Street caused the worst economic downturn in this country, and in fact the world, since the Great Depression. That's a fact. I know it's easy not to talk about it, but that is the fact.

Today six huge Wall Street financial institutions have assets equivalent to 60 percent of our GDP; close to $10 trillion. If Teddy Roosevelt, a good Republican, were alive today I know what he would say, and what he would say is that when you have six financial institutions issuing half the mortgages and two-thirds of the credit cards in this country, it is time to break them up, and I've introduced legislation to do just that.

In terms of health care, we have got to grapple, as I mentioned a moment ago, with the fact that we remain the only major country without a national health care program. I believe very strongly in a Medicare for all singer-payer system. Right now, in fact on

Wednesday, and I say this as the ranking member of the Budget Committee, my Republican colleagues are going to begin their effort to try to cut Social Security benefits. They're going to start off with disability benefits and go beyond that.

In my view at a time when senior poverty is increasing, when we have millions of seniors and I meet them in Vermont all the time; people are trying to get by on $12 - $14,000 a year. We should not be about cutting Social Security benefits. We should be about expanding those benefits.

As I mentioned a moment ago, we live in a time of massive wealth and income inequality, and we need a progressive tax system in this country which is based on ability to pay. It is not acceptable to me that a number of major profitable corporations have paid zero in federal income taxes in recent years, and that millionaire hedge-fund managers often enjoy an effective tax rate which is lower than truck drivers or nurses. It is absurd that we lose $100 billion a year of revenue because corporations and the wealthy stash their money in offshore tax havens like the Cayman Islands, Bermuda, and other places around the world. The time is now for real tax reform.

So, let me conclude by saying this. The struggle that we're in now is not just about protecting Social Security or Medicare or Medicaid or making college affordable to our kids or raising the minimum wage. It is something deeper than that. It is about whether we can put together a vibrant grass-roots movement all over this country which says to the billionaire class, "Sorry, government in this country is going to work for all of us and not just the top 1 percent." Thank you very much.

11

The Case for Democratic Socialism in the United States

Bhaskar Sunkara

Bhaskar Sunkara is founding editor of Jacobin *and publisher of* Catalyst: A Journal of Theory and Strategy. *He is author of* The Socialist Manifesto: The Case for Radical Politics in an Era of Extreme Inequality *(2019).*

In the following viewpoint, Bhaskar Sunkara praises Bernie Sanders's use of the term "democratic socialism" to positively identify and add substance to his political platform. As a candidate in the Democratic primary in 2020, Sanders's use of the label "socialism" turned out to be a liability, scaring off even many Democrats, who eventually selected centrist Democrat Joe Biden. Stances like Sanders's are embraced by many, including young voters, and threaten to splinter the Democrat Party.

In a speech yesterday at George Washington University in Washington, DC, the Vermont senator Bernie Sanders brilliantly articulated what he means when he calls himself a democratic socialist.

With characteristic concision, he decried the rule of "a small number of incredibly wealthy and powerful billionaires," and argued that the future belongs to either rightwing nationalism

"Bernie Sanders Just Made a Brilliant Defense of Democratic Socialism," by Bhaskar Sunkara, Guardian News & Media Ltd, June 13, 2019. Copyright Guardian News & Media Ltd 2020. Reprinted by permission.

or democratic socialism, which he defined as a bedrock set of economic and social rights.

Even for many sympathizers, Sanders' decision to call himself a socialist has always been controversial. The label strikes some as an anachronism—or even a liability, distracting from a broadly popular progressive vision. Americans, we are told, still fear the S-word and imagine breadlines and gulags when it's invoked.

But Sanders isn't among the most popular politicians in America despite his socialist past and identity—but because of it.

Sanders first found his ideology and political voice in the Young People's Socialist League, the youth section of the ailing Socialist Party of America. When Sanders joined in the 1960s, the party was a shell of what it was in the early 20th century, when Eugene V. Debs got almost a million votes for president and the party had hundreds of elected officials.

Even in its weakened state, however, American socialism was able to nurture and train Sanders. Through the movement, he came to an understanding of the world from which he has never departed: the rich aren't misguided; they have a vested interest in protecting their wealth and power and keeping millions of others at their mercy. We can't just design better policy—to build a more just world, we need to take power from the control of the rich and democratize it. With this awareness, Sanders, then a University of Chicago student, committed himself to the civil rights and labor struggles of the era.

Sanders' first forays into electoral politics were still on the fringes of American political life—as a 1972 Senate candidate for Vermont's leftwing Liberty Union party, he won just 2.2% of the vote. But his simple message reflected the moral clarity and vision of the old Socialist party: Richard Nixon represented "millionaires and billionaires," as Sanders said at the time, and propped up a "world of the 2% of the population that owns more than one-third of the personally held wealth in America."

We're used to politicians that vacilate, triangulate, "evolve." Sanders has done none of these things—he has maintained astounding message discipline for half a century. Inequality is undermining the promise of America, he has always argued, and a coalition of working people organizing against millionaires and billionaires can change things for the better.

Sanders still has a portrait of Debs in his Washington, DC, office, and in the 1980s he curated an album of the legendary socialist orator's speeches. But yesterday's address was a reminder that even though he still embodies much of the old socialist spirit, he has found ways to soften its edges and make it more accessible to ordinary Americans.

At George Washington University, Sanders once again railed against the billionaire class and "the profit-taking gatekeepers of our healthcare, our technology, our finance system, our food supply and almost all of the other basic necessities of life." But instead of citing his hero Debs, he drew on Franklin Delano Roosevelt—a president who saw himself as the liberal savior of the capitalist system. Yet in 1944, shortly before his death, Roosevelt put forth a sweeping manifesto he called the Second Bill of Rights. Existing political rights alone haven't given us "equality in the pursuit of happiness," Roosevelt argued; we need to complement those political rights by guaranteeing access to employment, housing, healthcare, education and more.

It was not socialism per se, but a blueprint for a social democratic safety net in the US—one that sadly never came to fruition.

By pointing to this history, Sanders is signaling that he's running to win the Democratic primary and the presidency. He aims to be the candidate of a party of governing power—the party of Roosevelt, not the party of Debs.

Yet beneath that signaling is a familiar appeal. Sanders' speech rooted democratic socialism in American soil, in popular desires for peace and security. He tied his analysis of the world—a coming conflict between the forces of rightwing populism and the progressive left, with no middle ground—with concrete demands for policies such as Medicare for All, a living wage and affordable housing.

For Democratic politicians like Joe Biden, social problems are complex and difficult to resolve. More often than not, there aren't any clearcut villains. As Biden put it recently: "The folks at the top aren't bad guys." For Sanders, they are—and they have names that he is unafraid to utter, such as the Walton and Trump families.

In his public speeches, Sanders criticizes the unequal present, identifies the people responsible for it, sketches out a more egalitarian future and specifies an agent of change ("working people") who can get us there. It's a simple socialist formula, communicated in simple language: Sanders was by far the most repetitive Democratic candidate in 2016 and continues to be today. He avoids jargon, and presents his socialism as common sense: a political revolution to take away power and wealth from the few and provide basic economic and social rights to the many.

Even if Sanders is still polling behind Biden, the message may be starting to resonate. Fifty-seven per cent of Democrats view socialism positively, along with 61% of those aged 18 to 24.

Yesterday, Sanders expanded his democratic socialist vision further, using the rhetoric of freedom that's a regular trope in American politics, but giving it a socialist gloss. "Political freedom in the absence of economic freedom is not real freedom."

Hardened socialists might scoff at Sanders's summoning of Roosevelt as a proto-socialist. But the core of his call for democracy and justice is true to the spirit of Debs and his successors Norm Thomas and Michael Harrington, and resonates with millions. Sanders isn't just campaigning, he's spearheading the recovery of an American tradition of democratic socialism that insists we expand our definition of freedom to include our most basic material needs.

12

Approaching Oligarchy in the Legal System
Rebecca Buckwalter-Poza

Rebecca Buckwalter-Poza is senior adviser at the Justice Collaborative. Previously she served as judicial affairs editor at Daily Kos and deputy national press secretary for the Democratic National Committee during the 2008 presidential election.

Oligarchy generally refers to economic forms of inequality. But in this viewpoint, Rebecca Buckwalter-Poza argues that the American justice system suffers from major structural inequalities and that these inequalities have created an oligarchy in the legal environment. In the United States, the burden of seeking justice falls to the individual. Unfortunately, parties in civil cases do not have a generalized right to counsel. In fact, in 75 percent of all US civil trial cases, at least one of the litigants has no lawyer. Worse, many Americans are unaware of their legal rights, and without legal advice they never even get to court to seek justice.

Access to justice is now more critical than ever. In the United States, Americans need a lawyer's help for everything from avoiding an unjust eviction to preventing a wrongful conviction. Yet, effective legal assistance remains out of reach for the majority of Americans. The gap between legal needs and the services available exacerbates systemic inequities and disadvantages that will only grow over the next four years. This series examines the state of

"Making Justice Equal," by Rebecca Buckwalter-Poza, Center for American Progress, December 8, 2016. Reprinted by permission.

access to justice in the United States and how public and private actors can join forces to make justice equal for all Americans.

For two years, Mary Hicks paid $975 per month for a run-down Washington, D.C., apartment. When she contacted the landlord about mold and mildew in the bathroom and holes in the walls, he did nothing. After Mary began to withhold rent, her landlord sued her.

Mary sought help from a law clinic. Her student attorneys not only kept her from being evicted and ensured that her landlord made the repairs but also reduced her rent to $480 after discovering that her unit was rent-controlled.[1]

Mary was fortunate. While 90 to 95 percent of landlords are represented by lawyers before the Landlord and Tenant Branch of the D.C. Superior Court, only 5 to 10 percent of tenants have legal assistance.[2] Unlike criminal defendants, parties in civil cases do not have a generalized right to counsel. While all states provide a right to counsel for at least a few types of civil cases, most parties in civil cases that involve high stakes and basic human needs, such as housing, do not have a right to representation.[3]

In more than three-fourths of all civil trial cases in the United States, at least one litigant does not have a lawyer.[4] Figures are even starker when it comes to family law, domestic violence, housing, and small-claims matters—those involving disputes over amounts up to $25,000, depending on the state. At least one party lacks representation in 70 to 98 percent of these cases.[5]

And these are just the Americans who make it to court. Without access to legal advice, many are unaware of their legal rights and potential claims. Past estimates and more recent state-by-state studies suggest that about 80 percent of the civil legal needs of those living in poverty go unmet[6] as well as 40 to 60 percent of the needs of middle-income Americans.[7] But because these figures depend upon self-selection and self-reporting, however, and because many Americans do not identify their unmet legal needs as such, it is impossible to estimate Americans' total unmet legal needs.[8]

To deny Americans access to legal assistance is to deny them their rights and protections. This is because, to a greater degree than other countries, the United States places the burden on an individual to seek justice by going to court.[9] Other developed democracies have enshrined the right to counsel in civil cases and devote 3 to 10 times more funding to civil legal aid than the United States.[10] In areas from environmental regulation and workplace discrimination to civil rights and housing, Americans must hire or find their own attorneys to enforce the law. The result is a divide between those who can afford legal assistance and those who cannot.

This issue brief is the first in a series that examines access to justice as a long-neglected policy concern integral to American democracy—one that is under threat from the coming administration.[11] It provides important information on the US justice gap and makes the case for prioritizing improvements in civil aid and indigent defense through legislative and infrastructure initiatives. It also outlines steps that state legislators, courts, and outside actors, such as advocacy organizations, can take to make justice equal.

Understanding the Justice Gap

The justice gap—that is, the gap between legal needs and services available—has the greatest implications for the United States' most vulnerable populations: those at greatest risk under the policies announced by the incoming administration.[12] On the civil side, people of color,[13] women,[14] immigrants,[15] the elderly,[16] people with disabilities,[17] and lesbian, gay, bisexual, and transgender, or LGBT, people[18] are more likely to live in poverty and more likely to need legal assistance. Claiming protections under the Americans with Disabilities Act, for example, often requires, at a minimum, legal advice, and at most, litigation.

The justice gap not only most affects those living in poverty but also perpetuates poverty. It also comes at great cost to government: Preventing eviction, for instance, is less expensive for governments than providing emergency housing or covering the higher costs associated with homelessness. In particular, providing attorneys for litigants in cases involving housing, health care, and domestic violence saves governments money and creates both social and economic benefits.[19]

In New York state, every dollar spent on civil legal aid creates $10 in benefits for the recipients of the assistance, their communities, and the state combined.[20] Likewise, North Carolina aid providers found that each dollar the state spends on legal aid yields $10 in economic benefits.[21] Montana[22] and Pennsylvania[23] have each seen a return on investment of $11 per dollar spent on legal aid.

In the criminal system, too, those who cannot afford an attorney are at a disadvantage—even with the constitutional right to representation. Terrence Miller met his court-appointed defense attorney for the first time on the morning of his first hearing on drug charges.[24] The attorney, who had not handled a criminal case in seven years, had been assigned to Miller's case only four days prior.[25] He was only able to speak to Miller for a few minutes.[26] Yet the judge denied the lawyer's requests for more time to prepare, and Miller was convicted in just a few days.[27] A New Jersey appellate court affirmed the conviction on the grounds that Miller failed to prove that the trial would have gone differently had he met his attorney earlier.[28]

In the last year for which the Bureau of Justice Statistics published detailed figures, more than 80 percent of felony defendants charged with violent crimes in the largest US counties could not afford to hire attorneys; the same was true for 66 percent of such defendants in US district courts.[29] Other estimates for the percentage of criminal cases involving indigent defendants nationwide put that figure as high as 90 percent.[30] Current funding and staffing levels for publicly funded lawyers cannot keep up with this demand. One estimate suggests that 6,900 more public defenders would be needed to manage the current caseload in the United States.[31]

Defendants with publicly appointed attorneys are more likely to be detained before trial as well as more likely to be jailed.[32] Facing time and resource limitations, publicly funded attorneys often resort to plea bargains: 90 to 95 percent of defendants represented by a public defender plead guilty.[33] People of color are disproportionately represented among those in poverty and in the criminal justice system due in part to racial profiling and bias at stages from investigation to prosecution. As a result, they are disproportionately disadvantaged by the failings of indigent defense systems.[34]

Over the past century, and even recently, Congress and the courts have achieved remarkable progress on civil rights, social welfare, and criminal justice through landmark legislation and rulings. But if the people for whom these rulings are meant to protect do not have access to civil legal aid or receive adequate defense representation, these protections become irrelevant to their daily lives.

Shortfalls in Civil Legal Aid

When Congress created the Legal Services Corporation in 1974,[35] it was responding to "a need to provide equal access to the system of justice in our Nation."[36] The Legal Services Corporation Act's sponsors noted that "providing legal assistance to those who face an economic barrier to adequate counsel will serve best the ends of justice and assist in improving opportunities for low-income persons."[37]

Today, the Legal Services Corporation is the biggest source of funding for civil legal aid for low-income Americans.[38] It funds programs that provide direct legal services in every state.[39] Legal aid lawyers help Americans meet everyday needs, including housing and health care. They also provide assistance in extreme circumstances, such as making sure that victims of 9/11 and the *Deepwater Horizon* oil spill in the Gulf Coast received benefits from government compensation funds.[40]

Unfortunately, in practice, too few Americans qualify for legal aid due to the extremely low income cutoff. In 2015, an individual had to make less than $14,713 per year—a family of four, less than $30,313 per year—to be eligible for Legal Services Corporation aid.[41] Americans making several times as much can ill afford to hire a lawyer, a luxury that runs $200 to $300 per hour on average.[42] The high cost of justice has a deterrent effect on even high-income individuals, who pursue legal action to resolve unpaid debts just 46 percent of the time.[43]

Worse, funding shortages mean that only half of those who are eligible for and seek legal aid get help.[44] While Legal Services Corporation programs aided 1.8 million Americans in 2013, another 1.8 million or more people were turned away.[45] And, of course, these figures underrepresent the scale of the problem because they only include cases in which help was sought and denied—not all those where help was needed.[46]

Congress has not only placed restrictions on who can receive aid but has also politicized how aid can be used. For example, just as the Hyde Amendment bars the use of federal funds to pay for abortion,[47] the Legal Services Corporation Act bars grantees from most abortion-related legal proceedings.[48] Legal Services Corporation-funded programs also cannot lobby government offices, agencies, or legislators—or take class-action cases.

As a result of congressional restrictions, legal aid attorneys are limited in what they can do to affect the overarching policies and institutions that foment and entrench injustice. And once a program accepts just $1 of Legal Services Corporation funding, it must adhere to these restrictions in all activities, even if it receives money from other, nonrestricted sources.[49]

Today, unmet legal needs are at an unacceptable level and growing as civil legal aid funding is shrinking.[50] Congressional appropriations for the Legal Services Corporation were just $385 million in 2016.[51] In the early 1980s, by contrast, the corporation received more than $770 million annually.[52] Adjusted for inflation, the corporation's budget has decreased by 300 percent since 1981, even as the number of Americans eligible for aid has grown by 50 percent.[53]

Beginning in 2009, the second-largest source of legal aid funding in the United States also began to decrease. Since 1980, all 50 states have created Interest on Lawyers Trust Account programs, or IOLTAs. These accounts fund legal aid with interest earned on client funds that lawyers temporarily deposit in a trust account.[54] In 2007, IOLTA income was more than $370 million. By 2008, however, it fell to $284 million, and, in 2009, it was just $92 million due to dropping interest rates.[55]

Some state IOLTAs have been more gravely affected than others. In North Carolina, the state IOLTA disbursed more than $4 million in grants in 2008 and 2009. In 2016, IOLTA grants came to just $2 million.[56] Texas, meanwhile, saw a staggering 80 percent decline in IOLTA revenue, from $20 million in 2007 to $4.4 million in 2012.[57]

Many IOLTA programs have attempted to mitigate losses by developing relationships with banks, asking for higher returns on their accounts in return for publicly acknowledging banks' assistance, and making lawyers' participation—and their use of the highest-yield account possible—mandatory.[58]

Some states are also exploring creative solutions for bolstering IOLTA revenues. In Indiana, legislators approved a $1 civil filing fee that will generate $450,000 for legal aid. The Indiana and Pennsylvania supreme courts have mandated that some portion of all unclaimed funds from class action lawsuits be directed to IOLTAs.[59] But these policies only help mitigate the effect of low interest rates on IOLTA programs.[60] It is also important for state legislatures to take steps to fund legal aid directly.

The Crisis in Indigent Defense

The Sixth Amendment requires that "[i]n all criminal prosecutions, the accused shall enjoy the right ... to have the assistance of counsel for his defense."[61] In *Gideon v. Wainwright*, the Supreme Court found the Sixth Amendment right to counsel to be fundamental, noting, "In our adversary system of criminal justice, any person … who is too poor to hire a lawyer, cannot be assured a fair trial unless counsel is provided for him. This seems to us to be an obvious truth."[62]

Nine years later, in *Argersinger v. Hamlin*, the Court clarified that this Sixth Amendment right to counsel applies in all criminal proceedings where the loss of liberty may be involved:

> Absent a knowing and intelligent waiver, no person may be imprisoned for any offense, whether classified as petty, misdemeanor, or felony, unless he was represented by counsel at his trial.[63]

Despite these words, many defendants who cannot afford counsel in the United States go unrepresented or do not receive adequate and meaningful representation.

In 2004, 41 years after the ruling in *Gideon*, the American Bar Association published a report titled "Gideon's Broken Promise," which concluded that "indigent defense in the United States remains in a state of crisis, resulting in a system that lacks fundamental fairness and places poor persons at constant risk of wrongful conviction."[64]

The nationwide crisis in indigent defense has its roots in inadequate funding at the state level. In 2016, the Missouri state public defender's office needed a budget increase of $23.1 million to represent indigent defendants in state court.[65] Gov. Jay Nixon (D) recommended an increase of just $1 million, leading to the director of the Missouri State Public Defender System's headline-making decision to highlight the shortfall by appointing the governor as a public defender.[66] The Missouri indigent defense system ranks 49th in the United States.[67]

Around the country, defendants find themselves represented by undertrained, unsupported, or overloaded defense counsel. Additional structural problems include courts failing to provide counsel as required by the Constitution or state law; prosecutors pushing defendants to waive the right to counsel or to plead guilty; and judges permitting or even soliciting deficient waivers of the right to counsel.[68] Some judges and elected officials even improperly exert influence over defense counsel. As a whole, the criminal justice system suffers from a lack of oversight and accountability.[69]

Although data on indigent defense systems are limited,[70] it is clear that this crisis has escalated since the *Gideon* ruling. Public defender programs are underfunded and overburdened. The gap between public defense capacities and need is only growing, yet from 2008 to 2012, total state government funding on public defense changed relatively little, ranging from $2.2 billion to $2.4 billion.[71] Nationwide, prosecutors' offices receive $3.5 billion more in funding than public defense budgets.[72]

Making Justice Equal

Making justice equal for all Americans must be a priority for the incoming administration, Congress, and state governments.

Congress must increase Legal Services Corporation funding, expand eligibility, and lift restrictions on aid. Legislators should begin by removing the so-called super restriction that limits Legal Services Corporation grantees' use of noncorporation funding. State legislatures must likewise increase funding for legal aid and, like Indiana, find ways to revive and support IOLTA programs. State supreme courts should follow Indiana and Pennsylvania in directing unclaimed class action awards to legal aid.

Ultimately, improving indigent defense systems requires state legislatures to increase funding for defender programs and improve infrastructure. Federal actors can help bridge the gap, however, by publicizing existing federal grants that public defenders can use to fund defense work and increasing congressional appropriations for additional grants.

Courts and outside actors also have roles to play. Judges should exercise their discretion to appoint attorneys more often and ensure that defenders have the opportunity to give the best defense possible. Courts can simplify legal processes and promote access to justice technology—such as educational applications—to make it easier for individuals to navigate the legal system on their own. Bar associations, law firms, and law schools can increase pro bono contributions and enact policies to improve access to legal services.

Finally, issue advocacy organizations working to protect and advance the interests of the people that the justice gap most affects—those living in poverty, people of color, women, immigrants, the elderly, people with disabilities, and LGBT people—must begin to address and prioritize access to justice. Equal access to legal representation in the justice system is critical to ending poverty, combating discrimination, and creating opportunity—especially now.

Endnotes

1. Mary Hicks, Testimony before the Council of the District of Columbia Committee on the Judiciary hearing on B21-0879, "Expanding Access to Justice Act of 2016," October 19, 2016.
2. Eric S. Angel and Beth Mellen Harrison, Testimony before the Council of the District of Columbia Committee on the Judiciary hearing on B21-0879, "Expanding Access to Justice Act of 2016," October 19, 2016.
3. John Pollock, "The Case Against Case-by-Case: Courts Identifying Categorical Rights to Counsel in Basic Human Needs Civil Cases," Drake Law Review 61 (2013): 763–815.
4. National Center for State Courts, "The Landscape of Civil Litigation in State Courts" (2015). See also, Jessica K. Steinberg, "Demand Side Reform in the Poor People's Court," Connecticut Law Review 47 (3) (2015): 741–807.
5. Deborah Rhode, Access to Justice (Oxford, UK: Oxford University Press, 2004).
6. Ibid.
7. Ibid; Legal Services Corporation, "The Unmet Need for Legal Aid."
8. Rebecca L. Sandefur, What We Know and Need to Know About the Legal Needs of the Public, 67 S. Car. L. Rev. 443, 453 (2016).
9. Deborah Rhode, Access to Justice.
10. Earl Johnson, "Lifting the 'American Exceptionalism' Curtain: Options and Lessons from Abroad," Hastings Law Journal 67 (2016) 1225–1264; World Justice Project, "Rule of Law Index 2015" (2015).
11. Republican Study Committee, "RSC Budget Options 2005" (2005).
12. Jane C. Timm, "The 141 Stances Donald Trump Took During His White House Bid," NBC News, November 28, 2016; Fortune, "Civil Rights Groups Sound the Alarm About the Trump Administration," November 15, 2016.
13. National Poverty Center, "Poverty in the United States"; Deborah Povich, Brandon Roberts, and Mark Mather, "Low-Income Working Families: The Racial/Ethnic Divide" (Washington: The Working Poor Families Project, 2015).
14. National Women's Law Center, "NWLC Analysis of 2014 Poverty Census Data," October 21, 2015.

Is America a Democracy or an Oligarchy?

15. Columbia Law School Human Rights Institute and Northeastern University School of Law Program on Human Rights and the Global Economy, "Equal Access to Justice: Ensuring Meaningful Access to Counsel in Civil Cases, Including Immigration Proceedings" (2014).
16. Juliette Cubanski, Giselle Casillas, and Anthony Damico, "Poverty Among Seniors: An Updated Analysis of National and State Level Poverty Rates Under the Official and Supplemental Poverty Measures" (Washington: Kaiser Family Foundation, 2015); Jeffrey D. Colman and Danielle E. Hirsch, "Increasing Access to Justice for the Elderly and Others: The Illinois Experience," Experience 24 (1) (2014).
17. Pam Fessler, "Why Disability and Poverty Still Go Hand in Hand 25 Years After Landmark Law," National Public Radio, July 23, 2015.
18. Legal Services NYC, "Poverty Is an LGBT Issue: An Assessment of the Legal Needs of Low-Income LGBT People" (2016); M.V. Lee Badgett, Laura E. Durso, and Alyssa Schneebaum, "New Patterns of Poverty in the Lesbian, Gay, and Bisexual Community" (Los Angeles: Williams Institute, 2013); Nico Sifra Quintana, "Poverty in the LGBT Community" (Washington: Center for American Progress, 2009).
19. Laura K. Abel and Susan Vignola, "Economic and Other Benefits Associated with the Provision of Civil Legal Aid," Seattle Journal for Social Justice 9 (1) (2010): 139–167.
20. Permanent Commission on Access to Justice, "Report to the Chief Judge of the State of New York" (2015).
21. UNC Center on Poverty, Work and Opportunity and NC Equal Access to Justice Commission, "A 108% Return on Investment: The Economic Impact to the State of North Carolina of Civil Legal Services in 2012" (2014).
22. Montana Legal Services Association, "The Economic Impact of Civil Legal Aid to the State of Montana" (2015).
23. Letter from Stephanie S. Libhart, executive director of the Pennsylvania Interest on Lawyers Trust Account Board, to James J. Sandman, president of the Legal Services Corporation, May 21, 2015.
24. *State of New Jersey v. Terrence Miller*, No. A-6243-07T4, Superior Court of New Jersey, Appellate Division (June 13, 2011).
25. Andrew Cohen, "How Much Does a Public Defender Need to Know About a Client?" The Atlantic, October 23, 2013.
26. Ibid.
27. *State of New Jersey v. Terrence Miller*.
28. Ibid.
29. Caroline Wolf Harlow, "Defense Counsel in Criminal Cases" (Washington: Bureau of Justice Statistics, 2000); Alexandra Natapoff, "Gideon's Silence," Slate, May 31, 2006.
30. Bureau of Justice Assistance, Contracting for Indigent Defense Services: A Special Report (US Department of Justice, 2000).
31. Ibid.
32. Ibid.
33. Ibid.
34. Rebecca Marcus, "Racism in Our Courts: The Underfunding of Public Defenders and Its Disproportionate Impact Upon Racial Minorities," Hastings Constitutional Law Quarterly 22 (1994): 219–267; Marc Mauer, "Justice for All? Challenging Racial Disparities in the Criminal Justice System," Human Rights 37 (4) (2010): 14–16.

35. Legal Services Corporation Act of 1974, Pub. L. No. 93–355, 88 Stat. 378 (1974).
36. Ibid.
37. Ibid.
38. Legal Services Corporation, "Who We Are."
39. Ibid.
40. Ibid.
41. Ibid.
42. Martha Bergmark, "We don't need fewer lawyers. We need cheaper ones," The Washington Post, June 2, 2015; Steven Davidoff Solomon, "Law Schools and Industry Show Signs of Life, Despite Forecasts of Doom," The New York Times, March 31, 2015.
43. Steven Seidenberg, "Unequal Justice: US Trails High-Income Nations in Serving Civil Legal Needs," ABA Journal, June 1, 2012.
44. Legal Services Corporation, "Documenting the Justice Gap in America: The Current Unmet Civil Legal Needs of Low-Income Americans" (2009).
45. Legal Services Corporation, "Who We Are."
46. Legal Services Corporation, "Documenting the Justice Gap in America."
47. Heidi Williamson and Jamila Taylor, "The Hyde Amendment Has Perpetuated Inequality in Abortion Access for 40 Years" (Washington: Center for American Progress, 2016).
48. Legal Services Corporation, "About Statutory Restrictions on LSC-funded Programs."
49. Brennan Center for Justice, "The Restriction Barring LSC-Funded Programs from Freely Using Their Non-LSC Money," June 20, 2001.
50. Deborah Rhode, Access to Justice.
51. Legal Services Corporation, "FY 2016 Spending Bill Increases Funding for LSC by $10 Million," Press release, December 18, 2015; Consolidated Appropriations Act, 2016, Pub. L. No. 114–113 (2015).
52. Rachel M. Zahorsky, "Everything on the Table: LSC Looks to ABA to Help Meet Legal Needs of the Poor," ABA Journal, January 1, 2012.
53. Memorandum from James J. Sandman, president of the Legal Services Corporation, to Finance Committee, "Management's Recommendation for LSC's FY 2017 Budget Request," July 13, 2015.
54. National Association of IOLTA Programs, "What Is IOLTA?"
55. Brennan Center for Justice, "Civil Legal Services: Low-Income Clients Have Nowhere to Turn Amid the Economic Crisis" (2010). The website maintained by the National Association of IOLTA Programs and the American Bar Association Commission on IOLTA asserts that, to the contrary of the Brennan Center's figures, "(I)n 2009, the US IOLTA programs generated more than $124.7 million nationwide." National Association of IOLTA Programs, "What Is IOLTA?"
56. North Carolina State Bar, "IOLTA Prepares to Make Grants with New Funding."
57. Robert J. Derocher, "The IOLTA crash: Fallout for foundations," Bar Leader 37 (1) (2012).
58. Ibid.
59. Ibid.
60. Ibid.
61. US Const. amend. VI.
62. 372 US 335, 344 (1963).
63. 407 US 25, 37 (1972).

64. American Bar Association Standing Committee on Legal Aid and Indigent Defendants, "Gideon's Broken Promise: America's Continuing Quest for Equal Justice" (2004).
65. Radley Balko, "Frustrated state public defender appoints Missouri Gov. Jay Nixon to represent indigent defendant," The Washington Post, August 4, 2016.
66. Ibid.
67. Letter from Michael Barrett, director of the Missouri State Public Defender System, to Gov. Jay Nixon, August 2, 2016.
68. American Bar Association Standing Committee on Legal Aid and Indigent Defendants, "Gideon's Broken Promise."
69. Ibid.
70. Erica J. Hashimoto, "Assessing the Indigent Defense System" (Washington: American Constitution Society, 2010).
71. Erinn Herberman and Tracey Kyckelhahn, "State Government Indigent Defense Expenditures, FY 2008–2012 – Updated" (Washington: Bureau of Justice Statistics, 2014. Note that this figure "may not be inclusive of county or jurisdictional appropriations for indigent defense."
72. Natapoff, "Gideon's Silence."

13

Labor Unions Still Matter in America
Jake Rosenfeld

Jake Rosenfeld is associate professor of sociology at Washington University in St. Louis. He is the author of What Unions No Longer Do (2014) *and the forthcoming* You're Paid What You're Worth: And Other Myths of the Modern Economy.

In this viewpoint, Jake Rosenfeld examines the declining power of organized labor in the United States and demonstrates how this decline has contributed to growing levels of economic and political inequality. In just 50 years, organized labor in the private sector fell from 35 percent to 6.5 percent. Organized labor is important for America's economic and civic health. Research has shown that a powerful labor movement results in increased wages for union members and non-members as well. Unions also narrow inequality for minority and immigrant workers, as well as bolstering civic participation such as voting.

The US labor movement was once the core institution fighting for average workers. Over the last half century, its ranks have been decimated. The share of the private sector workforce that is organized has fallen from 35% to approximately 6.5% today.

An expanding body of research demonstrates just what this loss has meant: the growth of economic and political inequality, stalled

"The Rise and Fall of US Labor Unions, and Why They Still Matter," by Jake Rosenfeld, The Conversation, March 27, 2015. https://theconversation.com/the-rise-and-fall-of-us-labor-unions-and-why-they-still-matter-38263. Licensed under CC BY-ND 4.0.

progress on racial integration and the removal of an established pathway for immigrant populations to assimilate economically.

Yet despite their decline, unions in the US retain some power in certain pockets of the country. Recent successes by these organizations reveal the importance of a revitalized labor movement for the nation's economic and civic health.

What Went Wrong?

By the mid-1950s, unions in the US had successfully organized approximately one out of every three non-farm workers. This period represented the peak of labor's power, as the ranks of unionized workers shrank in subsequent decades.

The decline gained speed in the 1980s and 1990s, spurred by a combination of economic and political developments. The opening up of overseas markets increased competition in many highly organized industries. Outsourcing emerged as a popular practice among employers seeking to compete in a radically changed environment. The deregulation of industries not threatened by overseas competition, such as trucking, also placed organized labor at a disadvantage as new nonunion firms gained market edge through lower labor costs.

Simultaneously, US employers developed a set of legal, semi-legal and illegal practices that proved effective at ridding establishments of existing unions and preventing nonunion workers from organizing. Common practices included threatening union sympathizers with dismissal, holding mandatory meetings with workers warning of the dire consequences (real or imagined) of a unionization campaign and hiring permanent replacements for striking workers during labor disputes.

A sharp political turn against labor aided these employer efforts. President Reagan's public firing of striking air traffic controllers vividly demonstrated to a weakened labor movement that times had changed. Anti-union politicians repeatedly blocked all union-backed efforts to re-balance the playing field, most recently in 2008-2009, with the successful Senate filibuster of the Employee Free

Choice Act. EFCA would have made private sector organization efforts somewhat easier. The last major piece of federal legislation aiding unions in their organization efforts passed in 1935.

Why Does It Matter?

At its peak, the US labor movement stood alongside powerful business leaders and policymakers as key institutions shaping the nation's economy and polity. Union workers enjoyed healthy union "wage premiums," or increases in pay resulting directly from working under a union-negotiated contract.

But nonunion workers also benefited from a strong labor presence.

In research by Harvard University's Bruce Western and myself, we compared nonunion workers in highly organized locales and industries to nonunion workers in segments of the labor market with little union presence. After adjusting for core determinants of wages, such as education levels, we found that nonunion workers in strongly unionized industries and areas enjoyed substantially higher pay. Thus the economic benefits of a powerful labor movement redounded to unorganized workers as well as union members.

Early 20th-century unions—especially craft unions—engaged in a range of sometimes violent discriminatory practices. As a result, in 1935, the year that President Franklin Roosevelt signed the Wagner Act, less than 1% of trade unionists were African American. While the Wagner act extended basic organizing rights to private sector workers, millions of minorities remained unable to enjoy its protections by the actions of unions themselves. But throughout the second half of the 20th century, many unions shed these racist and xenophobic legacies.

In so doing, they opened up their organizations to African Americans eager to escape explicitly racist policies and practices common to many nonunion workplaces. African Americans soon had the highest organization rates of any racial or ethnic group, peaking at more than 40% for African American men and nearly 25% for African American women in the private sector.

These exceptional organization rates helped narrow racial pay disparities by raising African American wages. Had no union decline occurred from the early 1970s on, black-white wage gaps among women would be between 13% and 30% lower, and black males' weekly wages would be an estimated US$50 higher. Meanwhile, many immigrants and their children, echoing pathways taken by newcomers in generations past, such as the predominantly female, predominantly immigrant population of the International Ladies' Garment Workers' Union (ILGWU), used the labor movement as a springboard into the nation's middle class.

Unions' equalizing impact was not limited to the economic realm. A large body of research has found that union membership spurs civic participation among non-elite Americans. Voting, for example, is a practice strongly graded by income and education. More of either and Americans are much more likely to turn out to vote. Unions helped to counteract class-based inequality in political participation, ensuring that elected officials heard the policy desires of millions of non-elite Americans.

What Now for Labor?

The labor movement now finds itself in a peculiar period.

On the one hand, ongoing attacks by anti-union forces have crippled unions' organizational models in what were labor strongholds, including Wisconsin and Michigan. Many of these attacks have taken dead aim at what remains of labor's real strength: its public sector membership base.

Abetted by recent court decisions, efforts to defund and defang public sector unions are growing in size and sophistication by right wing policymakers and lobbying groups.

Curiously, despite serving as a primary source of votes and finances for the Democratic Party for much of the 20th Century, labor finds itself with few political allies.

On the other hand, unions have enjoyed a series of recent successes at the state and local level. Movements to raise the minimum wage, offer paid sick leave to employees and pressure the largest private sector employer—Walmart—to raise its base compensation have all, of late, succeeded. These victories can be attributed, in part, to labor unions.

Unions provided much of the organizational and financial support that helped deliver these victories to millions of working Americans. Yet none of these wins translate directly into new dues-paying members.

Further successes on behalf of America's working- and middle-class appear limited unless unions discover a means to maintain its funding base. And without a revitalized labor movement, it is likely our inequality levels will remain at record highs.

14

Populism Is No Match for the Elite Establishment

Dan Sanchez

Dan Sanchez is the director of content at the Foundation for Economic Education (FEE) and the editor-in-chief of FEE.org.

Donald Trump campaigned for the presidency—and was elected—as a candidate for the people. However, not long into his single term, he mostly abandoned the pledges he'd made to his supporters. What happened? Written less than one year into Trump's time in office, this viewpoint argues that the populist president didn't stand a chance against the establishment machine of Washington, DC, politics. The author claims that it is inevitable that all political organizations succumb to "the iron law of oligarchy."

Did the Deep State deep-six Trump's populist revolution? Many observers, especially among his fans, suspect that the seemingly untamable Trump has already been housebroken by the Washington, "globalist" establishment. If true, the downfall of Trump's National Security Adviser Michael Flynn less than a month into the new presidency may have been a warning sign. And the turning point would have been the removal of Steven K. Bannon from the National Security Council on April 5.

"Trump Surrenders to the Iron Law of Oligarchy," by Dan Sanchez, Foundation for Economic Education, May 1, 2017. https://fee.org/articles/trump-surrenders-to-the-iron-law-of-oligarchy/. Licensed under CC BY 4.0.

Until then, the presidency's early policies had a recognizably populist-nationalist orientation. During his administration's first weeks, Trump's biggest supporters frequently tweeted the hashtag #winning and exulted that he was decisively doing exactly what, on the campaign trail, he said he would do.

In a flurry of executive orders and other unilateral actions bearing Bannon's fingerprints, Trump withdrew from the Trans-Pacific Partnership, declared a sweeping travel ban, instituted harsher deportation policies, and more.

These policies seemed to fit Trump's reputation as the "tribune of poor white people," as he has been called; above all, Trump's base calls for protectionism and immigration restrictions. Trump seemed to be delivering on the populist promise of his inauguration speech (thought to be written by Bannon), in which he said:

> *Today's ceremony, however, has very special meaning. Because today we are not merely transferring power from one administration to another, or from one party to another—but we are **transferring power from Washington, D.C., and giving it back to you, the American People.***
>
> *For too long, a small group in our nation's Capital has reaped the rewards of government while the people have borne the cost. Washington flourished—but the people did not share in its wealth. Politicians prospered—but the jobs left, and the factories closed.*
>
> ***The establishment protected itself, but not the citizens of our country.*** *Their victories have not been your victories; their triumphs have not been your triumphs; and while they celebrated in our nation's capital, there was little to celebrate for struggling families all across our land.*
>
> *That all changes—starting right here, and right now, because this moment is your moment: it belongs to you.*
>
> *It belongs to everyone gathered here today and everyone watching all across America. This is your day. This is your celebration. And this, the United States of America, is your country.*
>
> *What truly matters is not which party controls our government, but whether our government is controlled by the people. January 20th 2017, will be remembered as the day the*

people became the rulers of this nation again. *The forgotten men and women of our country* will *be forgotten no longer.*
   Everyone is listening to you now. [Emphasis added.]

After a populist insurgency stormed social media and the voting booths, American democracy, it seemed, had been wrenched from the hands of the Washington elite and restored to "the people," or at least a large, discontented subset of "the people." And this happened in spite of the establishment, the mainstream media, Hollywood, and "polite opinion" throwing everything it had at Trump.

The Betrayal

But for the past month, the administration's axis seems to have shifted. This shift was especially abrupt in Trump's Syria policy.

Days before Bannon's fall from grace, US Ambassador to the UN Nikki Haley declared that forcing Syrian president Bashar al-Assad from power was no longer top priority. This too was pursuant of Trump's populist promises.

Trump's nationalist fans are sick of the globalist wars that America never seems to win. They are hardly against war per se. They are perfectly fine with bombing radical Islamists, even if it means mass innocent casualties. But they have had enough of expending American blood and treasure to overthrow secular Arab dictators to the benefit of Islamists; so, it seemed, was Trump. They also saw no nationalist advantage in the globalists' renewed Cold War against Assad's ally Russian president Vladimir Putin, another enemy of Islamists.

The Syrian pivot also seemed to fulfill the hopes and dreams of some anti-war libertarians who had pragmatically supported Trump. For them, acquiescing to the unwelcome planks of Trump's platform was a price worth paying for overthrowing the establishment policies of regime change in the Middle East and hostility toward nuclear Russia. While populism wasn't an unalloyed friend of liberty, these libertarians thought, at least it could be harnessed to sweep away the war-engineering elites. And since war is the health of the state, that could redirect history's momentum in favor of liberty.

But then it all evaporated. Shortly after Bannon's ouster from the NSC, in response to an alleged, unverified chemical attack on civilians, Trump bombed one of Assad's airbases (something even globalist Obama had balked at doing when offered the exact same excuse), and regime change in Syria was top priority once again. The establishment media swooned over Trump's newfound willingness to be "presidential."

Since then, Trump has reneged on one campaign promise after another. He dropped any principled repeal of Obamacare. He threw cold water on expectations for prompt fulfillment of his signature promise: the construction of a Mexico border wall. And he announced an imminent withdrawal from NAFTA, only to walk that announcement back the very next day.

Here I make no claim as to whether any of these policy reversals are good or bad. I only point out that they run counter to the populist promises he had given to his core constituents.

"The forgotten men and women of our country" have been forgotten once again. Their "tribune" is turning out to be just another agent of the power elite.

Who yanked his chain? Was there a palace coup? Was the CIA involved? Has Trump been threatened? Or, after constant obstruction, has he simply concluded that if you can't beat 'em, join 'em?

The Iron Law of Oligarchy

Regardless of how it came about, it seems clear that whatever prospect there was for a truly populist Trump presidency is gone with the wind. Was it inevitable that this would happen, one way or another?

One person who might have thought so was German sociologist Robert Michels, who posited the "iron law of oligarchy" in his 1911 work *Political Parties: A Sociological Study of the Oligarchical Tendencies of Modern Democracy*.

Michels argued that political organizations, no matter how democratically structured, rarely remain truly populist, but inexorably succumb to oligarchic control.

Even in a political system based on popular sovereignty, Michels pointed out that "the sovereign masses are altogether incapable of undertaking the most necessary resolutions." This is true for simple, unavoidable technical reasons: "such a gigantic number of persons belonging to a unitary organization cannot do any practical work upon a system of direct discussion."

This practical limitation necessitates delegation of decision-making to office-holders. These delegates may at first be considered servants of the masses:

> All the offices are filled by election. The officials, executive organs of the general will, play a merely subordinate part, are always dependent upon the collectivity, and can be deprived of their office at any moment. The mass of the party is omnipotent.

But these delegates will inevitably become specialists in the exercise and consolidation of power, which they gradually wrest away from the "sovereign people":

> The technical specialization that inevitably results from all extensive organization renders necessary what is called expert leadership. Consequently the power of determination comes to be considered one of the specific attributes of leadership, and is gradually withdrawn from the masses to be concentrated in the hands of the leaders alone. Thus the leaders, who were at first no more than the executive organs of the collective will, soon emancipate themselves from the mass and become independent of its control.
>
> Organization implies the tendency to oligarchy. In every organization, whether it be a political party, a professional union, or any other association of the kind, the aristocratic tendency manifests itself very clearly.

Trumped by the Deep State

Thus elected, populist "tribunes" like Trump are ultimately no match for entrenched technocrats nestled in permanent bureaucracy. Especially invincible are technocrats who specialize in political force and intrigue, i.e., the National Security State (military, NSA, CIA, FBI, etc). And these elite functionaries don't serve "the people" or any large subpopulation. They only serve their own careers, and by extension, big-money special interest groups that make it worth their while: especially big business and foreign lobbies. The nexus of all these powers is what is known as the Deep State.

Trump's more sophisticated champions were aware of these dynamics, but held out hope nonetheless. They thought that Trump would be an exception, because his large personal fortune would grant him immunity from elite influence. That factor did contribute to the independent, untamable spirit of his campaign. But as I predicted during the Republican primaries:

> …while Trump might be able to seize the presidency in spite of establishment opposition, he will never be able to wield it without establishment support.

No matter how popular, rich, and bombastic, a populist president simply cannot rule without access to the levers of power. And that access is under the unshakable control of the Deep State. If Trump wants to play president, he has to play ball.

On these grounds, I advised his fans over a year ago, "…don't hold out hope that Trump will make good on his isolationist rhetoric…" and anticipated "a complete rapprochement between the populist rebel and the Republican establishment." I also warned that, far from truly threatening the establishment and the warfare state, Trump's populist insurgency would only invigorate them:

> Such phony establishment "deaths" at the hands of "grassroots" outsiders followed by "rebirths" (rebranding) are an excellent way for moribund oligarchies to renew themselves without actually meaningfully changing. Each "populist" reincarnation of the

power elite is draped with a freshly-laundered mantle of popular legitimacy, bestowing on it greater license to do as it pleases. And nothing pleases the State more than war.

Politics, even populist politics, is the oligarchy's game. And the house always wins. For the people, the only winning move is not to play.

Organizations to Contact

The editors have compiled the following list of organizations concerned with the issues debated in this book. The descriptions are derived from materials provided by the organizations. All have publications or information available for interested readers. The list was compiled on the date of publication of the present volume; the information provided here may change. Be aware that many organizations take several weeks or longer to respond to inquiries, so allow as much time as possible.

American Enterprise Institute
1789 Massachusetts Avenue NW
Washington, DC 20036
(202) 862-5800
website: www.aei.org

Founded in 1943, the American Enterprise Institute (AEI) is a research and advocacy organization dedicated to promoting democracy, free enterprise, and American global leadership. AEI scholars conduct research in a wide variety of fields, including economics, education, health care, and foreign policy.

American Institute for Economic Research
PO Box 1000
Great Barrington, MA 01230-1000
(888) 528-1216
email: info@aier.org
website: www.aier.org

Founded in 1933, the American Institute for Economic Research (AIER) is dedicated to educating Americans on ideals including free trade, property rights, and limited government. AIER publishes research, hosts colloquiums, and sponsors scholarship, and is home to the Bastiat Society and the Sound Money Project.

Americans for Financial Reform
1615 L Street NW, Suite 450
Washington, DC 20036
(202) 466-1885
email: info@ourfinancialsecurity.org
website: https://ourfinancialsecurity.org

Americans for Financial Reform is a nonpartisan and nonprofit coalition of more than 200 civil rights, consumer, labor, business, investor, faith-based, and civic and community groups. Formed in the wake of the 2008 crisis, it is working to lay the foundation for a strong, stable, and ethical financial system.

Brookings Institution
1775 Massachusetts Avenue NW
Washington, DC 20036
(202) 797-6000
email: communications@brookings.edu
website: www.brookings.edu

With over 300 academic and government experts, the Brookings Institution is one of the premier policy think tanks in the United States. Brookings experts conduct research on foreign policy, economics, development, and governance, and provide policy recommendations based on that research.

Center for American Progress
1333 H Street NW, 10th Floor
Washington, DC 20005
(202) 682-1611
website: www.americanprogress.org

The Center for American Progress (CAP) is a liberal-leaning think tank focused on economic issues in the United States, including income inequality, tax policy, and education. With an extensive communications and outreach infrastructure, CAP works to ensure that progressive ideals are represented in the national political conversation.

Economic Policy Institute
1225 Eye Street NW, Suite 600
Washington, DC 20005
(202) 775-8810
email: epi@epi.org
website: www.epi.org

The Economic Policy Institute (EPI) is a nonpartisan organization focused on spotlighting the interests of low and middle income workers in policy discussions that typically focus on the interests of the investment class. EPI also develops policy proposals aimed at increasing working class security and productivity.

European Centre for International Political Economy
Avenue des Arts 40, 1040
Brussels, Belgium
email: info@ecipe.org
website: www.ecipe.org

The European Centre for International Political Economy (ECIPE) is an independent, nonprofit think tank dedicated to the study of European economic issues. ECIPE advocates for free trade and the progressive reduction of economic barriers as a path toward greater peace, prosperity, and security across the globe.

FactCheck.org
Annenberg Public Policy Center
202 S. 36th St.
Philadelphia, PA 19104-3806
(215) 898-9400
email: editor@factcheck.org
website: www.factcheck.org

FactCheck.org is a nonpartisan, nonprofit "consumer advocate" for voters that aims to reduce the level of deception and confusion in US politics. It monitors the factual accuracy of what is said by major US political players in the form of TV ads, debates, speeches, interviews, and news releases.

Independent Voter Project
PO Box 34431
San Diego, CA 92163
(619) 207-4618
email: contact@independentvoterproject.org
website: www.independentvoterproject.org

The Independent Voter Project (IVP) is a nonprofit, nonpartisan (501(c)4) organization dedicated to better informing voters about important public policy issues and to encouraging nonpartisan voters to participate in the electoral process.

National Constitution Center
Independence Mall
525 Arch Street
Philadelphia, PA 19106
(215) 409-6600
website: www.constitutioncenter.org

The National Constitution Center is the first and only institution in America established by Congress to "disseminate information about the United States Constitution on a non-partisan basis in order to increase the awareness and understanding of the Constitution among the American people." The Constitution Center brings the United States Constitution to life by hosting interactive exhibits and constitutional conversations and inspires active citizenship by celebrating the American constitutional tradition.

National Democratic Institute
455 Massachusetts Avenue NW, 8th Floor
Washington, DC 20001-2621
(202) 728-5500
website: www.ndi.org

The National Democratic Institute is a nonprofit, nonpartisan, nongovernmental organization that has supported democratic institutions and practices in every region of the world for more than three decades. Since its founding in 1983, NDI and its local partners have worked to establish and strengthen political and civic organizations, safeguard elections, and promote citizen participation, openness, and accountability in government.

Peterson Institute for International Economics
1750 Massachusetts Avenue NW
Washington, DC 20036
(202) 328-9000
email: comments@piie.com
website: www.piie.com

The Peterson Institute for International Economics (PIIE) is a private, nonpartisan think tank dedicated to the study of economics, trade policy, and globalization. PIIE conducts research on emerging issues, develops policy ideas, and works to educate government officials, business leaders, and the public on international economic issues.

Pew Research Center
1615 L Street NW, Suite 800
Washington, DC 20003
(202) 419-4300
website: www.pewresearch.org

Pew Research Center is a nonpartisan fact tank that informs the public about the issues, attitudes, and trends shaping the world. It conducts public opinion polling, demographic research, media content analysis, and other empirical social science research. Pew Research Center does not take policy positions.

PolitiFact
1100 Connecticut Avenue NW
Suite 440
Washington, DC 20036
(202) 463-0571
website: www.politifact.com

PolitiFact is a fact-checking website that rates the accuracy of claims by elected officials and others who speak up in American politics.

World Economic Forum

350 Madison Avenue, 11th Floor
New York, NY 10017
(212) 703-2300
email: forumusa@weforum.org
website: www.weforum.org

The World Economic Forum is a nonprofit organization based in Geneva. It is focused on facilitating public-private cooperation and policy agreement in the interest of promoting a healthy and stable global economic environment.

World Trade Organization

Centre William Rappard
Rue de Lausanne, 154
Case postale
1211 Genève 2
Switzerland
email: enquiries@wto.org
website: www.wto.org

The Geneva-based World Trade Organization (WTO) is an international organization that facilitates trade policy agreements and helps to resolve disputes between nations. Its goal is to promote a smooth, predictable, and competitive global trade environment.

Bibliography

Books

Kurt Andersen. *Evil Geniuses: The Unmaking of America: A Recent History.* New York, NY: Random House, 2020.

Andrea Bernstein. *American Oligarchs: The Kushners, the Trumps, and the Marriage of Money and Power.* New York, NY: W. W. Norton & Company, Inc., 2020.

Ron Formisano. *American Oligarchy: The Permanent Political Class.* Chicago, IL: University of Illinois Press, 2017.

Chrystia Freeland. *Plutocrats: The Rise of the New Global Super Rich and the Fall of Everyone Else.* New York, NY: Penguin Books, 2013.

Anand Giridharadas. *Winners Take All: The Elite Charade of Changing the World.* New York, NY: Alfred A. Knopf, 2018.

Garett Jones. *10% Less Democracy: Why You Should Trust Elites a Little More and the Masses a Little Less.* Stanford, CA: Stanford University Press, 2020.

Christopher Leonard. *Kochland: The Secret History of Koch Industries and Corporate Power in America.* New York, NY: Simon & Schuster, 2019.

Nancy MacLean. *Democracy in Chains: The Deep History of the Radical Right's Stealth Plan for America.* New York, NY: Penguin Books, 2017.

Jane Mayer. *Dark Money: The Hidden History of the Billionaires Behind the Rise of the Radical Right.* New York, NY: Anchor Books, 2016.

Jane McAlevey. *No Shortcuts: Organizing for Power in the New Gilded Age.* New York, NY: Oxford University Press, 2016.

George E. Monroe. *Hidden Enemies of Democracy: Oligarchies on the Rise.* Bloomington, IN: Authorhouse, 2019.

Robert Reich. *The System: Who Rigged It, How We Fix It.* New York, NY: Alfred A. Knopf, 2020.

Michael Sandel. *The Tyranny of Merit: What's Become of the Common Good?* New York, NY: Farrar, Straus, and Giroux, 2020.

Joseph E. Stiglitz. *The Price of Inequality: How Today's Divided Society Endangers Our Future.* New York, NY: W. W. Norton & Company, Inc., 2013.

Zephyr Teachout. *Break 'Em Up: Recovering Our Freedom from Big Ag, Big Tech, and Big Money.* New York, NY: St. Martin's Publishing Group, 2020.

Periodicals and Internet Sources

John Cassidy, "Is America an Oligarchy?" *New Yorker*, April 18, 2014. https://www.newyorker.com/news/john-cassidy/is-america-an-oligarchy

Ashley Fisher, "Don't Call America a Democracy, Call It a Plutocracy," *Daily Evergreen*, April 25, 2014. https://dailyevergreen.com/3903/opinion/dont-call-america-a-democracy-call-it-a-plutocracy/

Akbar Ganji, "The Transformation of American Democracy to Oligarchy," *Huffpost*, August 6, 2015. https://www.huffpost.com/entry/the-transformation-of-ame_1_b_7945040

Patrick J. Kiger, "What Is an Oligarchy and Has the US Become One?" How Stuff Works, May 20, 2019. https://people.howstuffworks.com/oligarchy.htm

Joel Kotkin, "What Do the Oligarchs Have in Mind for Us?" *Quillette*, June 19, 2019. https://quillette.com/2019/06/19/what-do-the-oligarchs-have-in-mind-for-us/

Andrew Levine, "Oligarchy in America," CounterPunch, March 31, 2017. https://www.counterpunch.org/2017/03/31/oligarchy-in-america/

Dylan Matthews, "Remember That Study Saying America Is an Oligarchy? 3 Rebuttals Say It's Wrong," Vox, May 9, 2016. https://www.vox.com/2016/5/9/11502464/gilens-page-oligarchy-study

Nicholas Misukanis, "American Oligarchy: How the South Won the Civil War," *Commonweal Magazine*, June 23, 2020. https://www.commonwealmagazine.org/american-oligarchy

Carole Owens, "Is America Becoming an Oligarchy?" *Berkshire Edge*, April 23, 2019. https://theberkshireedge.com/connections-32/

Robert Reich, "America's Real Divide Isn't Left vs. Right. It's Democracy vs. Oligarchy," *American Prospect*, July 6, 2019. https://prospect.org/economy/america-s-real-divide-left-vs.-right.-democracy-vs.-oligarchy/

Heather Cox Richardson, "America in Crisis: How 'We the People' Saved Democracy from Oligarchs in 1850, 1890, and 1920," *Milwaukee Independent*, March 3, 2020. http://www.milwaukeeindependent.com/articles/america-crisis-people-saved-democracy-oligarchs-1850-1890-1920/

Luke Savage, "America Is an Oligarchy. It Doesn't Have to Be," *Jacobin Magazine*, February 15, 2019. https://www.jacobinmag.com/2019/02/us-oligarchy-wealthy-billionaires-democracy

Manisha Sinha, "The Oligarchs' Revenge," *Nation*, October 19, 2020. https://www.thenation.com/article/culture/heather-cox-richardson-how-south-won-civil-war-review/

Ganesh Sitaraman, "Countering Nationalist Oligarchy," *Democracy: A Journal of Ideas*, Winter 2019. https://

democracyjournal.org/magazine/51/countering-nationalist-oligarchy/

Anne Sraders, "What Is an Oligarchy and What Does It Mean in 2019?" TheStreet, August 3, 2018. https://www.thestreet.com/politics/what-is-an-oligarchy-14671881

Jeffrey A. Winters, "Oligarchy and Democracy," *American Interest*, September 28, 2019. https://www.the-american-interest.com/2011/09/28/oligarchy-and-democracy/

John W. York, Ph.D., "No, America Is Not an Oligarchy Run by the Ultra-Rich," The Heritage Foundation, July 7, 2017. https://www.heritage.org/poverty-and-inequality/commentary/no-america-not-oligarchy-run-the-ultra-rich

Index

A
Amadeo, Kimberly, 8, 11–16
Anderson, Sarah, 58–68
Argersinger v. Hamlin, 95

B
Bauer, Peter, 30
Biden, Joe, 87
Blair, Tony, 34
Boudreaux, Donald, 29
Brandeis, Louis, 24
Brazil, 61
Buckwalter-Poza, Rebecca, 88–100

C
Calvino, Italo, 32
campaign funding/donations, 8, 14
Capital in the Twenty-First Century, 57
capitalism, explanation of, 26
Captured: The Corporate Infiltration of American Democracy, 52, 56
Cavanagh, John, 58–68
Center for Responsive Politics, 63
Chevron, 59, 67
China, 11, 23, 70, 75
Citizens United v. FEC, 53, 54, 81
Clinton, Bill, 34
Clinton, Hillary, 37
Cohen, David, 15
Continental Resources, 14
Coolidge, Calvin, 48

D
DaimlerChrysler, 59, 61, 62, 66, 67
dark money, 54, 55
Dawes, Charles, 47
democracy, explanation of, 7, 25–26, 29
Democratic Party/Democrats, 14, 15, 17, 18, 32, 33, 34, 35, 37, 45, 71, 81, 86, 87, 104

E
economic mobility, 8, 36
Enron, 59, 67
Exxon Mobil, 61, 62

F
Ford, Henry, 51
Foulkes, Arthur, 25–30
France, 61
Fujitsu, 66

G

General Electric, 62
General Motors, 59, 60, 62, 67
Germany, 61, 82
Gideon v. Wainwright, 94–95, 96
Gilded Age, 9, 23
Gore, Al, 60
Great Compression, 20
Great Depression, 19–20, 21, 48, 57, 82
Great Divergence, 21
Great Recession, 21
Griffith, D. W., 50

H

Hacker, Jacob, 8
Hamilton, Alexander, 27
Hamm, Harold, 14
Harding, William G., 48
Hewlett-Packard, 66
Higgs, Robert, 29
Holcombe, Randall G., 26
Hoover, Herbert, 48
Hungary, 31

I

IBM, 62, 66
Icahn, Carl, 56
income/wealth inequality, 8, 13, 14, 15, 17–21, 22–24, 29, 31–41, 77–83
India, 23, 61
Institute on Taxation and Economic Policy, 67
Interest on Lawyers Trust Account programs (IOLTAs), 94, 96
International Labor Organization, 66
International Monetary Fund, 61
Iran, 11
"iron law of oligarchy," 12
Israel, 61

J

Japan, 61, 66
Jefferson, Thomas, 27, 53
Johnson, Jake, 69–76
Johnston, Matthew, 17–21
judicial inequality, 88–97

K

Kennedy, Liz, 52–57
King, Willford I., 18
Koch, Charles and David, 14, 81
Kolko, Gabriel, 28

L

labor unions/union membership, 19, 20–21, 101–105
League of Nations, 47
Legal Services Corporation, 92–93, 96–97
liberal neutrality, 39, 40–41
Lippman, Walter, 42
Lipton, Eric, 56
Loewentheil, Nathaniel, 8

M

Macron, Emmanuel, 23
Madison, James, 27, 28
marginal tax rates, 18–19, 20, 21
McKesson, 59, 67
Michels, Robert, 109–110
Mitsubishi, 66
Mueller, Robert, 32
Murray, William H., 18

N

NEC, 66
Necessary and Proper clause, 27
New Deal, 19, 27, 47
Nineteenth Amendment, 9, 45

O

Obama, Barack, 34–35, 37, 82
Occupy Wall Street, 15, 35, 79
oligarchy, explanation of, 8, 11

P

PepsiCo, 59, 67
Piketty, Thomas, 18, 57
Pilon, Roger, 27–28
Pirie, Madsen, 30
plutocracy, explanation of, 12
Poland, 31
populism, 9, 15, 18, 31–41, 106–112
Progressive Era, 9, 10, 28

R

Reagan, Ronald, 33–34, 102
Republican Party/Republicans, 14, 15, 34, 48, 71, 78, 81, 82, 83, 111
Rodgers, Daniel T., 9, 42–51
Roosevelt, Theodore, 44–45, 53–54, 82
Rosenfeld, Jake, 101–105
Royal Dutch/Shell, 62
Russia, 11, 23, 31, 32, 57, 74, 108

S

Saez, Emmanuel, 18
Sanchez, Dan, 106–112
Sandel, Michael, 31–41
Sanders, Bernie, 15, 35, 69–76, 77–83, 84–87
Saudi Arabia, 11
Schroeder, Gerhard, 34
Sony, 62, 66
South Africa, 11, 61
South Korea, 61
Sunkara, Bhaskar, 84–87
super PACs, 14, 54
Sussman, S. Donald, 15

T

Taft, William Howard, 46
Tea Party, 15, 35, 79
Tenth Amendment, 27
Texaco, 59, 67
Thatcher, Margaret, 33

Trump, Donald, 15, 23, 31–33, 35, 37, 39–40, 55–56, 87, 106–112
Turkey, 11, 31

U
Unheavenly Chorus, 55

W
Walmart, 62, 67, 80, 105
Washington, George, 27
Wenders, John, 27, 30
Western, Bruce, 103
Whitehouse, Sheldon, 52, 53, 54, 55, 56
Wilson, Charles, 60
Wilson, Woodrow, 45, 47
women's suffrage, 9, 45, 50
World Bank, 61, 63
Worldcom, 59, 67
World Inequality Report, 22
World War I, 19, 46, 47, 49

5